The Hazard for Spies

Hearts in Hazard / Book 11

by

M.A. Lee

WRITERS INK BOOKS

The Hazard for Spies
Copyright © 2020 Emily R. Dunn /
Doing Business as M. A. Lee & Writers' Ink

First electronic publishing rights: April 2020

NOTE FROM THE AUTHOR

This book is a work of fiction. The names, characters, places, and incidents are products of the writer's imagination or have been used fictitiously and are not to be construed as real. Any resemblance to persons, living or dead, actual events, locale or organizations is entirely coincidental. The author does not have any control over and does not assume any responsibility for third-party websites or their content

Published in the United States of America
Cover Illustration by Deranged Doctor Design

www.writersinkbooks.com
winkbooks@aol.com

Books by M.A. Lee

Fiction

The Hearts in Hazard series
A Game of Secrets
A Game of Spies
A Game of Hearts

The Dangers of Secrets
The Dangers for Spies
The Dangers to Hearts

The Key to Secrets
The Key for Spies
The Key with Hearts

The Hazard of Secrets
The Hazard for Spies
The Hazard with Hearts

Into Death Trilogy with Isabella Newcombe

Digging into Death
Christmas with Death
Portrait with Death

Non-Fiction for Writers

Think like a Pro Writer series
Think like a Pro ~ 1
Think / Pro: A Planner for Writers ~ 2
Old Geeky Greeks: Write Stories with Ancient Techniques ~ 3

Discovering Your Novel ~ 4
Discovering Characters ~ 5
Discovering Your Plot ~ 6
Discovering Your Author Brand ~ 7
Discovering Sentence Craft ~ 8

Just Start Writing ~ Inspiration 4 Writers 1

Table of Contents

Acknowledgements

This story didn't want to come together. Before I started preparation for this *Hazard for Spies*, I knew the protagonists' conflict and relationship arcs. I knew the two chief antagonists. I knew the secondary protagonist and the side characters. Maybe that was the problem ~ knowing too much of the story before writing began. But ~ I always know this much of any story before I begin.

Perhaps the story difficulties arose from a reluctance to say "farewell" to the original conflict in the first three books: ordinary people struggling against spies and smugglers and other nefarious individuals. A few characters from those first three novels recur in *The Hazard for Spies*, one as an active participant, others merely mentioned.

My troubles may have come from outside sources. Life rolls were occurring, switching the bits and pieces of every day around. None were out of control, but they created a disquietude whenever I wanted to sink into the writing.

Whatever the reason, when the words began flowing, *The Hazard for Spies* became a story that greatly pleased me as both a writer and a reader. The **Hearts in Hazard** series is nearing conclusion. Words for the twelfth book in the series, *The Hazard with Hearts,* are flowing, a strong current pouring into the future.

Writers live in made-up worlds, converse with fictitious people, fight invented battles, and solve imaginary mysteries. We are able to immerse ourselves in those interior worlds because of supportive people. Several times I have credited Diane and Steve, who encouraged every one of my earliest steps into professional writing and still offer that circle of support.

For this book, however, I specifically want to thank my niece Audrey. No matter the stresses and events, she maintains serenity. No matter the circumstance, she offers kindness to everyone. No matter the grind of the day-to-day world, she still believes an imaginary world can become real.

For Audrey, a great soul
who teaches me much more
than I have ever taught others.

London
31 August to 2 September 1814

Chapter 1

A hand dropped on Vic's shoulder. He stopped scratching his picks through the lock's resisting tumblers.

The round moon cast her silvery eye over the alley. Soon she would drift beyond the narrow walkway between the buildings. The silvery light would travel with her, leaving the alley dark except for the golden gleams peeking through the cracks of Elise's shuttered lantern.

Her light hand lifted from his shoulder, and he returned to his work, figuring out the tumblers on the heavy lock safeguarding the warehouse side door.

She bent close, her breath a warm wisp across his cheek. "How much longer? That's the third pass by the watchman."

"Nearly there," he lied. He didn't know if he could get past this lock, rusted after long months in rain and cold. He fumbled for a heavier pick.

She huffed, and Vic knew she hadn't believed him.

Times like this, the job chancy and the watchman vigilant, Vic missed the known of Liverpool. The escape routes, the likeliest hiding places, refuges from stout fists, the constable who would turn eyes elsewhere. He didn't like London's crowded buildings and sooty streets, the seething markets, the constant noise even in the deeps of night. He'd stay, though, till they found the information that Elise and her aunt Phinney hunted.

The strong wire pick Bessy worked past Hook and Fine to reach the last tumbler, stiff with rust. Vic gave a jerky twist. The tumbler resisted then "creached", the word Ollie had taught him for the soft screech of metal giving way to his picks. As the lock swung from its shackle, he caught it, cold in his hand, rough with rust.

Elise snatched up the shuttered lantern. Her sharp elbow moved him aside. The door opened into darkness with a glow of light off to their left. That was street-side, where the front office would be. The light lured the unwary, but Vic knew better than to head for it, for the light meant watchmen resting between their patrols.

High windows admitted the moonlight. The silvery radiance might illuminate the night sky, but they would need stronger light to find their way through the warehouse. Stacked crates formed haphazard walls, and piled on and around them were boxes, trunks, and barrels, too many to count.

Elise glided over the bricked floor, smoothed by years of use. She didn't open the lantern shutters, but light streamed around the metal plates, joined badly, repaired worse, but still better than candlelight that would signal a watchman. Cautious skittering started off to his left. Rats, the big London ones that stared before running to hide, considering attack rather than flight. A good mouser would have a battle against London rats.

She reached back, grabbed his coat, and hauled him inside. He shut the door gently.

"Lock?" she hissed.

"Pocket."

She dragged him a few steps before Vic planted his feet. "Come on," she demanded.

"Where to?" he retorted, keeping his voice equally low. "Can't see nothing."

"We'll use the lantern upstairs. The windows are shuttered there."

"Steps or ladder?" He didn't like ladders. Rickety things weren't kept in repair until someone fell and died.

Elise snorted, "Stairs. In the middle," but she didn't sound sure.

"This the right warehouse?" he questioned, not for the first time.

"Come on," she ordered, and he followed because she still had his coat bunched in her fist.

Elise had explained her plan on the day after they arrived in London, almost ten days ago. Her aunt Phinney was off talking to her friend, the matron who offered them rooms in her mission. Hank had hared off to the kitchens, pretending to focus on fresh scones. Emissary to the house, he brought back all snippets of unusual information. In less than a day he had formed an instant friendship with the cook, a lean African woman that Vic had trouble understanding but who turned out food better than he'd ever had in his short life.

Drawing Vic to the double entry for the residence quarter of the mission, Elise sat him on the floor beneath the coats to lay out her plan. She claimed her father had had a second office where he kept important documents. She sketched a plan to find the building on a Church Garden Street near the river. They would break in at night then go through the documents until she found her father's murderer.

Vic listened. He saw problems with the girl's plan, not least that they were little more than children and they would be running the London streets when the criminals were about. He didn't anticipate that she had the street name wrong. That problem took a week of cautious questions to discover it was Kirkgardie rather than Church Garden. Then they discovered the street ran a long ways beside the river. More days were lost walking and searching. More days passed before Elise spotted the blocky building with its unpainted plank walls warping in London's moist air. "That's it!" she cried then clapped her hand over her mouth.

No one had heard her. That was luck. They scouted round, counting windows, locating doors. Vic liked the narrow side door with its thick rusting lock, proof that few people paid any attention to the door. He didn't like the watchmen patrolling the exterior. More men would be inside, that he knew, but her elation infected him. He scouted for a couple of days and a couple of evenings on his own, learning the men's routines, before he agreed to break into the warehouse.

Neither of them mentioned anything to Phinney. They didn't want the young woman to worry. She would be frantic if Elise or Hank went missing. Vic came up with a good story in case she questioned him. But Phinney hadn't noticed. She'd been gone herself. "A job," she told them at breakfast, "cleaning offices. We should pay Mrs. Stowbridge something for taking us in, giving us rooms and food. I'll be working in law offices near the Old Bailey."

Vic thought nothing of it.

Elise stared at her boiled egg like it turned her stomach. "Which lawyers?"

"You wouldn't know them, dear."

"Papa was a lawyer here in London before he moved to Liverpool, only a few months before he and Mama—died."

Phinney bit into her scone. It crumbled, and she caught the pieces in an open hand. "Yes, Rosie wrote me. Peter was in London more than at home. Did you wish to go to his old office?"

"No. He closed that office." Her blue eyes met Vic's.

"I remember," her aunt said, still chasing crumbs. "Rosie said that he had opened the office in Liverpool where his primary client was based. Everything else was stored at the house in Merrybush." She sipped her tea. Lifting the quilted cozy, she picked up the teapot and offered to warm the children's cups before re-filling hers.

"Which lawyers are in the building, Aunt Phinney?"

"I suppose you might know them, especially after our stay at Parton March. The ground floor is all clerks, of course, and reception. A large firm of barristers has the entire first floor. Clements, Pickard, and Quincy. Do you know that firm?" After Elise shook her head, Phinney set aside her teacup. She named other firms housed on the second floor. Her eyes tracked an invisible line. "Third floor. Phipps and LaVesque. Titterstone and Montjoy. Fulbright."

Vic's mind stopped at Titterstone and Montjoy. Those two were at Parton March when the murders and attempted murders had occurred and been solved. Titterstone was the mustached man who had ordered another man to kill Joe and Button. Joe had hired Vic to break into a locked office in Liverpool. An office from which Elise had taken a file.

And now he was sliding over the worn bricks, following Elise deeper into the warehouse, to break into her father's office and read more files.

She walked fearlessly along a side aisle, and he gradually made out a flight of stairs leading up. The warehouse was like a huge cave, with moonlight filtering through windows higher than a second floor. Riverside, though, was a balcony running the building's length. One steep flight of steps climbed to the balcony, and the silvery light revealed doors opening off the elevated walkway. The rooms that opened off the walk overlooked the Thames. Vic remembered those windows with their weathered shutters. None opened to admit good daylight.

Beneath the balcony were deeper shadows, more scratching rats. He didn't want to go there. He tried to gauge how far along they were. The warehouse had one massive door opening to the street and a long dock to load cargo into a boat.

Vic slowed as they neared the stairs. "You sure?" he asked as the steps creaked under them. Even in the darkness the floor looked a long way down. "Don't seem like the place for an office."

Moonlight shone on her pale face, glinted in her sun-yellow hair. "I remembered."

He wouldn't argue with memory.

Elise was ten, two years younger than him. He didn't know how she remembered something from when she was only eight. Hank was eight and couldn't remember nothing unless his sister drilled him on it. Sitting in the dark double entry, coats brushing their heads, the floor cold under his rump, he had listened to her plan to find the warehouse, creep into her father's old office, and discover the reason her parents were killed.

Vic didn't point out that this office could be closed, the documents removed, the furniture sold in the two years since her parents' deaths. That's what had happened to her father's office in Liverpool. He just agreed to help.

Yet he worried about the watchmen and the documents Elise planned to read. He worried about Phinney cleaning the offices of Titterstone and Montjoy, on the same hunt as her niece to find who had killed Peter and Rosie DeChambeaux.

And Joe and Button were now dead, because they broke into an office in Liverpool.

Killed by a man hired by the lawyer Titterstone.

. ~ . ~ . ~ .

Phinney tucked a dark tress back under the ruffled mobcap that topped her disguise as a cleaning maid.

Light glowed down the hall in a side office. While no one was present, someone obviously worked late. A clerk from the ground floor, she had guessed as she picked up crumbled paper that had missed the dustbin. She smoothed out the documents that had a clerk working into the small hours then folded them and tucked them into a pocket for later perusal.

The other offices needed only a cursory cleaning. She used the master key given her by Mr. Gregory to re-lock each office as she finished. "Never can be too careful, not with lawyers and their documents," the older man had said, his esses whistling through a missing tooth. "You keep everything locked good and tight, Mrs. Coates."

Phinney had nodded and accepted the key with a solemn promise to keep it on her person.

She didn't grin at this unexpected luck until Mr. Gregory headed off to deal with a creaking shutter.

Her luck continued to hold. She had only the two top floors to clean while Mrs. Gregory took the bottom two. Mr. Gregory fixed problems, did the heavy work, and maintained the cellars with its large coal bin.

As she slipped into the offices of *Titterstone & Montjoy, Solicitors*, she gave a fleeting thought to the children, sleeping soundly at the mission. She had tucked up Hank then reminded Elise to put aside her reading before the downstairs clock struck the eighth hour. Bright blue eyes sparkling with mischief, her niece complained but acquiesced. Vic had a primer and pencil, working on the alphabet that Elise was trying to teach him.

Vic might not be family, but he formed part of their little family now, the three children and her, alone against the world.

Vic had warned them to flee from Liverpool. After trouble with press gangs, Phinney hadn't hesitated to hustle them onto the first coach out of the city. The boy had then protected their journey to Parton March. Once they were settled, seemingly safe, Phinney had tried to leave the children at the estate. She hadn't reached the neighboring village before she demanded the carter return her to the house. She couldn't leave them with strangers, even if the strangers seemed trustworthy.

Now she stood in the offices of *Titterstone & Montjoy*, convinced the two upstanding attorneys were criminals.

She had lucked into the job as cleaner. Mr. Gregory accepted her disguise as a war widow desperate to support her three children.

At Parton March, she had avoided any interaction with the two lawyers, there to serve their wealthy client as he determined his heirs. Even with murder and attempted murder, she kept herself and the children closeted, well away from the family and guests. She knew of George Titterstone and Kennedy Montjoy from Rosie's correspondence. Her sister poured out in a letter that Peter's father had involved himself in another *contretemps* on a business venture. In resolving the issue, the son had fallen out with his father and severed the connection when they left London.

Phinney only vaguely remembered those months before her sister and brother-in-law were killed. Working as a governess of four children had consumed all her energies. She barely had a half-hour each day to herself. Her meals were taken with the children. Her employer required daily reports of the children's progress and weekly proof of that progress. The older girl was a dreamer; the twin boys were pranksters who preferred fishing and roaming to Latin and ciphers, and the youngest girl would sneak to the kitchen for a sweet from the cook. She had tucked Rosie's letter in her reticule and forgotten it—until she drew it out at the Lintons.

She shook herself mentally. Brown studies were an indulgence. She had offices to search.

A whisk over the surfaces with her duster, then she carried her lamp into Mr. Titterstone's inner office. Last night she had searched Mr. Montjoy's office. She wanted one document with Peter's name or even his father's, Pierre DeChambeaux. One document, to prove she was on the right track.

The kneehole desk had six drawers, three on each side. Mr. Titterstone had double-framed windows at his back. His partner had only one window and the smaller of the two offices. Mr. Montjoy's window view, however, looked toward the park at the end of the block. On a fine day he would see treetops and catch glimpses of flowers. Mr. Titterstone overlooked the street and the red-bricked building across the way, yet he had an inner closet with a narrow bed, washbasin, and shelving for boxed documents.

George Titterstone also worked more cases than his partner. A dozen labelled boxes were stacked on shelves to one side of the room. Phinney eyed those case files and wondered how long a perusal of each would take. She might need several nights to work through all of the files.

Tucking her cleaning basket with rags and wax polish beside the shelves, she approached the desk, choosing Mr. Titterstone's side. She quickly scanned the stacked ledgers and the documents inside folders, careful not to disarrange them. Her father hadn't liked any of his papers moved, especially when he prepared a sermon. Phinney had picked up items, dusted underneath, then replaced them, all without the Rev.

Darracott spotting the removals. Finding nothing, she tugged on the center drawer. It didn't budge. Slipping fingers under her mobcap, she withdrew two hair picks and set to work on the simple lock, mentally thanking Vic for his lessons.

When the clock in the outer office chimed the half-hour, Phinney climbed from her aching knees and glared at the desk. Nothing. Not a single paper with the name *DeChambeaux*. Only a couple of files had dates preceding the carriage accident, but those were innocuous statements about an estate called Ridings in Little Houghton, inherited by Sir Charles Audley from his uncle. Mr. Titterstone had jotted a half-page of notes about the classics scholar who was decoding Egyptian hieroglyphs from the Rosetta Stone. Three words in a different hand appended the note: *Poutaine, cipher, key.*

She slipped the note back into the file box, telling herself the intervening years would have resolved any issue. Yet those three words niggled at her as she searched the other drawers. Hands on her hips, she considered retrieving it, yet even as she reached for the drawer, the door to the outer office opened. Hurriedly, she grabbed up a cleaning cloth.

When Titterstone's office door opened, Phinney stayed crouched beside her basket and pretended to dust the bottom shelf.

"Here. Who are you?"

She straightened. Without looking in the man's direction, she bobbed a curtsey. "The cleaner, sir."

"I hadn't—you are here alone."

Phinney stiffened. "The Gregorys are below, sir," she snipped. "This floor is my duty. And the one below."

"It can't be."

At the confusing comment, Phinney chanced a look to see a tall, broad-shouldered man, black hair and pale skin, blue eyes so pale they looked like tinted glass. Her mouth dropped open.

Conrad Hoppock laughed. "It *is* you."

Chapter 2

Life kept surprising Conrad. Phinney Darracott in a maid's mobcap that hid her dark curls was a welcome surprise, one of the few. Her piquant features had the same archness as nine years before. An engulfing apron hid her slender frame. While his star had been ascendant, though, hers had plummeted after her father's death. Governess, he remembered. *Now a maid cleaning offices?*

Conrad wiped away his grin. "Josephine Elizabeth Darracott, I never expected to see you."

"Again? I think I heard an *again*."

His lips twitched, wanting to stretch wide. Phinney might be down, but she remained plucky. "*Never* I said. And meant it."

"You expected I would remain in Brize Norton until I dried up like a wheat crop left unharvested, all brown and useless."

"No, Phinney. No!" Rather than impress this girl who had once fascinated him, he had offended her. "I returned to Brize Norton a couple of years ago. My condolences on the deaths of your parents."

Her mobile mouth twisted. "I was gone by then, working as a governess until my sister—." She stopped. Her visible swallow hurt his own throat.

"I heard that, too. Your sister had a child, didn't she?"

"Two. Elise and Henry. Hank, we call him."

"They're with you?"

"Of course!" Her gaze dropped to the rag in her hand then swept around the office. "You work for *Messieurs* Titterstone and Montjoy?"

He hesitated only a second then told the official lie. "I clerk for them. I'm working on a brief now."

"That's your lamp burning in the side room down the hall?"

"Yes." He didn't know what else to say. "Are you—?"

Voices came from the hallway, muffled by the outer door he'd had the sense to shut.

"Oh, no," she whispered.

A key scraped in the lock.

He quickly pressed the inner door nearly shut then grabbed Phinney's arm and her lamp. She squeaked as he hustled her to the closet. "Open it."

She obeyed, as eager as he to hide.

He crowded behind her into the closet and yanked the door shut as the men's voices came louder. They had entered the anteroom. Conrad blew out the lantern and set it away from the door.

At the plunge into darkness, Phinney squeaked again and grabbed his arm. He clapped a hand over her mouth as light gleamed along the cracked door. He shifted a little, hoping for a view of the room.

Phinney staggered and grabbed his forearm. She pushed at his smothering hand. "Sh-h," he warned before he removed it. The gleam of light illuminated her pale face. Those large expressive eyes were closed. Her lips were parted. He wanted to kiss her—a stupid wish, really, with men coming into Titterstone's office. Yet that old desire pushed him. Well aware of the distance between a plow boy and the vicar's daughter, his fifteen-year-old self had controlled the yearning. He didn't want the vicar's cane planted across his back. The desire's resurgence didn't surprise him—but his job demanded he discover whom Titterstone met after-hours. That was as much a deterrent as the vicar's macassar cane.

He looked away from temptation and peered through the thin crack between door and jamb. He could see Titterstone's desk. The man must have brought in a candle, for the light jumped around as if a breeze wisped over the flame.

"You threw your lot in with the wrong people," the lawyer said. A creak came, and Conrad saw him turn his chair and sit.

Grey superfine wool entered his line of sight. "I never expected Napoleon to lose." A man's sleeve. Not as tall as him, for the shoulder was well below Conrad's eye-level.

"What do you want, sir? Do take that chair. How may I assist you? What are your needs?"

"This isn't a need; it's a necessity. I must return to my life here in England."

The man moved. Conrad saw the desk with its stack of ledgers, the array of files, loose papers strewn over the blotter. The inkwell gleamed like champagne in the shifting candlelight.

"Sir, how is your return to England possible? Too many people know you. The Westover family, especially Lord Alex who once counted you a dear friend. Lord Costell, who has recently inherited. The Wilsons, the Armitage brothers. These men move throughout society."

"They continue to drink the elixir of privilege while I inhabit drafty garrets and rat-infested apartments. I weary of being the foreigner that everyone can identify and of whom they attempt to take advantage. That life is no longer for me. I will return here to live."

"I do not advise it."

"Come, Titterstone, advice is not what I seek. Possibilities are. I appreciate your and Mr. Montjoy's efforts to keep me from being tried *in absentia*. On my return I need not live in the cream of society. I can inhabit the shadows ... as my uncle does."

Conrad sifted through the snippets of information, trying to divine the man's identity. Alex Westover had a friend named James Costell. The brothers Michael and Lucas Armitage walked the fringes of society, accepted in the tonniest ballrooms but also familiar with the gaming dens and streets of blue ruin. They worked for London's spycatcher, Sir Roger Nazenby. *That* name wasn't widely known.

This man—who was he? When had he fled England? What crime had sent him to the Continent?

"My uncle does very well for himself," the man said, and Conrad realized that he had missed Titterstone's reply. Phinney stood statue-still against him, barely breathing, her fingers still clutching his arm.

The chair creaked. Titterstone's arm rested on the blotter.

Phinney angled her head, trying to see more. Conrad tightened his hold, wanting to draw her away from the door.

"You would be content with that shadowy life?" The lawyer played with a letter knife, lifting it to turn and slide through his fingers only to turn it again and let the tip land in the blotter. "You should consult the Boss, not me."

The Boss? Did he mean the Boss of London? The man who ruled the criminal underworld?

Talk of a shadowy life now made sense.

Another creak, a different sound than the lawyer's chair. "The thing is, Titterstone, I owe my uncle a great debt. Not a monetary one. A debt that is much more difficult to repay. He will not support my plans until I repay him. He wants everything equaled out."

"I am well acquainted with the Boss of London and his idea of equaling debts. I am not, however, in the business of intangible usury, Mr. Malbury. I will work with you on tangible debts."

"*Intangible* usury? You sound like the lawyer you are, Titterstone. I do not expect you to advance me any funds. Neither does my uncle. He definitely does not need more money."

"I do not think—."

"My father is in ill health." The younger man rode over the lawyer's protest, calm words that still plowed ahead like an ox working up a muddy hill. "My uncle's message to me, notifying me of his steady decline, prompted my return. At the appropriate time, this office can ensure the estate's funds will be funneled to me. You and Montjoy do still retain my letter of intent to that effect." He paused, and Titterstone must have nodded, for he continued, "At the appropriate time, I will provide this office with my new location and my new name. Neither is yet decided. I am not the imbecile you believe that I am."

After he had turned the letter opener several times, Titterstone cleared his throat. "Your father may recover."

"Not according to my uncle."

"Have you seen him?"

"My father? Of course not. White Hall has agents watching their residence, as if they think I am foolish enough to walk brazenly to the front door. Three years since my departure, and they still watch the house."

"I meant, have you seen your uncle? Have you spoken with him about your return?"

"Ah, therein lies the rub, doesn't it? You and Montjoy have attempted to conceal your connection to Boss Malbury and other nefarious rulers, such as the master of Liverpool."

Titterstone dropped the letter opener. "I have had no contact—."

"My uncle knows that you were in Liverpool a few weeks ago. He knows the reason. He is curious about the contents of that file taken from a certain solicitor's office near the waterfront. A file that he knows you were so intent on concealing that you required Stevens to kill the two men who broke into that office for you. Joe and Button. Or did you bother to learn their names?"

Phinney jerked and began trembling.

His arm still around her shoulders, Conrad braced her against his chest. He stared at the mobcap ruffle that blocked his view of her face. *What does she know about Liverpool and two murdered men?* Information about those murders would please Chief Constable Evans. Not only could Titterstone be connected to murders by the assassin Stevens, but the theft of this file offered another avenue of inquiry. Yet Phinney apparently knew something about the theft and those two murders. His chief would want her interrogated. Conrad didn't want to.

I've just found her. I'll lose her again.

"What does Boss Malbury want?" the lawyer demanded. Rather than be quelled by Malbury's information, he had stubbed up like an ox that refused to plow another furrow. "What is this intangible usury he demands? For me to help you to the Malbury estate?"

A young Malbury, whose past misdeeds required that he live on the fringes of high society—for the Westovers and Costells were great names. Nephew of the great Boss Malbury, himself a shadowy figure of the London underworld, wielding enough power and influence that he skated free of any chains the London constabulary managed to sling around his subordinates. This Malbury had fled three years ago, running from charges that would have come from White Hall—.

Richard Malbury. The name roared out of the shadowy corners of Conrad's memory. He had fled England hours ahead of constables intent on arresting him for his role in a French spy ring. He was suspected of taking government despatches and giving them to a French *émigré*. Proof was lacking—until Robert LeBrun wrote a full confession the evening before his execution. Conrad himself had accompanied the officers who arrested Claude Thierry based on that confession.

Malbury had escaped. Thierry still wasted in a cell. The French spy ring had collapsed—only for another to take its place, a ring more vicious and lethal than Thierry's simple information-gathering operation.

Boss Malbury had a connection to the French spies through his nephew Richard.

The London boss likely had more contacts with the new spies, the ones who would have helped Richard Malbury flee England for the continent.

What does Boss Malbury want? became a very interesting question.

Richard Malbury had left his chair. Titterstone turned, an elbow now on the desk. When Conrad shifted a little right, he could see an edge of that grey superfine sleeve beside the far wall. From previous visits to this office, he could envision the muddy-colored landscape on the wall, the black lines of the Thames bridge above the river in flood, the sky a cloudy mixture of grey tinged with cream and tan and odd touches of green.

"Does he want money?" Titterstone asked, his hope obvious in the uplift of his voice.

Malbury chuckled. Conrad caught a glimpse of red brocade, a vivid reminder that only a door, partially opened, separated them from discovery. Phinney jerked again. Her hand lifted. Her fingers pressed to her mouth, as if she fought to hold back words.

"I told you, no. Nothing that tangible or that easy."

"What then?"

"Loose ends knotted up. Especially since those loose ends will never benefit him."

"Loose ends? Never benefit? What are you talking about?"

"When my uncle sent me to your firm, he depended upon you to look after my interests as well as you look after his."

"Trust me, sir, neglect has not interfered with our efforts on your behalf." He paused. Malbury didn't speak. The lawyer's chair creaked. "Since Napoleon abdicated and was exiled to Elba, the worry over French spies is decreasing. A year, no more than two, and then I can advise you to return to England. You must still remain in the shadows, as you call it. Even with this new peace, White Hall wants additional battles to win. They will scoop up all the spies they have managed to scope out. Many on the Continent are currently in disarray. Wait a few months longer, sir. Your association with Claude Thierry and Madame Sourantine and Robert LeBrun will gradually be forgotten. When the time is right, I can disentangle your name, the name of a British peer, from theirs.

"Of course," and his chair creaked as he rocked it, "you will never recoup your former standing. Too many influential people remain arrayed against you. The new Lord Westover is still incensed that you escape prosecution. His father lost his White Hall position because he clearly had not properly secured the red boxes from which you took the secret despatches. Lord Costell has become a vocal member of the House of Lords. He will not want a reminder that a former friend associated with French spies. Your other friends, indeed Lord Hargreaves himself, all are highly regarded, sir. Time will fade their memories. Time will be your friend."

Phinney had shifted at the recitation of Malbury's old friends. Conrad personally knew only the Costells, who owned the estate near Brize Norton. He wondered if she were remembering the bazaars and fairs hosted on the estate grounds. Of the other names, he recognized only Westover, for the young lord had been a rising backbencher in Parliament until his father's death last year.

Caught by the lawyer's words, like a closing argument to a jury, Conrad had merely followed the logic without considering those words and their impact on Richard Malbury. Now he shook his head at Titterstone's blindness. Malbury didn't want to return to his refugee status. He was determined to repay whatever intangible usury that his uncle demanded. Titterstone, urging "a little more time", ignored the evidence of Malbury's own words.

"This is an interesting painting," the younger man said, his back once more to the lawyer and the closet where they hid. "Quite an unexpected view. The river rushing along. The sky in turmoil above. They say paintings reflect the owner's personality, yet this is not my view of you, not at all. All of these hidden colors. Hidden motives, perhaps? I understand you have turned over several of your cases to Montjoy. That surprises me."

"Montjoy would counsel you the same as I have. Wait a little longer before you risk a return."

"Yes, I do not doubt that would be his counsel."

"You listen to both of us. We cover all cases, sir. Montjoy knows the nobs while I—."

"As you know my uncle and his ilk. Learn to listen, Titterstone. I said that my uncle sent me to you."

"Yes, sir, when you fled England—."

"No. This very afternoon, when I met with him to discover what he would require. He's not much for familial loyalty. Our kinship won me the meeting, that's all."

"I don't understand."

"My uncle needs loose ends knotted up. I told you that."

"Yes. Of course. Certainly it never does to leave any evidence dangling—."

"What was in that file? Evidence?"

"File?"

"The one you had stolen in Liverpool?"

"I'm not—."

"Where is that file? Come, Titterstone, tell me now."

"Sir." The chair scraped back. "That's not needed. Put it away, sir. I beg you."

At Titterstone's panic, Conrad pushed Phinney away, getting her away from the door and beside the thicker wall with its shelves. Only one thing would overset a lawyer: a threat to his safety. Even after years of arresting some contrary criminals, Malbury's rapid change from conversation to lethal threat shocked Conrad.

"Sir! Accidents can happen. We might have to call a surgeon."

"Or an undertaker." Malbury chuckled. "Calm, Mr. Titterstone. Have you ever seen the effect a dueling pistol has at close range? This close—less than four feet, I would judge—the bullet penetrating your flesh will be quite destructive."

"Threats are not necessary!"

"The file. Now."

"Mr. Malbury, sir, that file contains nothing that concerns your uncle. Or you."

"He wishes to judge that. Where do you have it? Here?" Papers floated into Conrad's view and vanished, landing silently on the polished floor. "Not there. Where are you looking? The eyes are always traitors. Tell me."

"I don't know what loose ends Mr. Malbury thinks I have. Or evidence. The file doesn't concern him. He can't be linked to this in any way. It's two years past."

"No? Then let me present the file to him. He can judge."

"My client's interests—."

"Do not coincide with my uncle's. Which do you think is deadlier?"

"Mr. Malbury, please, put that pistol away."

"Not in these ledgers, I think," and bound books thumped to the floor. More papers whisked up into Conrad's view then slowly settled. "Does Montjoy know about this file?"

"He is my partner. Our diverse interests—."

"Yes or no?" The long barrel of the dueling pistol entered his view. Malbury had extended his arm, closing the distance between pistol and victim. Titterstone had to be no more than two feet from the weapon. "Does Montjoy know the reason you went to Liverpool?"

"Y-yes."

"Does he know the contents of the file?"

"The file concerns the two of us. We made the decision—."

"The two of you and no one else? Yet you said 'my client's interests'. That means another person is aware of this file. Who?"

"To reveal the names—."

"More than one, then. Who are they?"

Backed into a corner by the pistol's threat, Titterstone reacted as he had earlier, bulldog stubborn. "A dead man cannot interest your uncle," he growled.

Phinney flew back to Conrad's side. Only his blocking arm kept her from reaching the door.

"A dead man is still only one man. You said *names*. Plural."

"I fear the wine with our dinner has scattered my wits. I intended to say *name*. Singular. The name of a dead man. You do not intend to shoot me, Mr. Malbury."

A shadow darkened the papers remaining on the blotter. Titterstone's raised arm, as if his hand would stop a bullet. Conrad tried to tow Phinney away from the door, but she clung to him, listening as if the names were more important than the danger of Malbury's pistol.

"Who is this dead man?"

"Peter DeChambeaux."

Phinney shoved at Conrad and reached for the door. He snatched her arm down. She struggled against him as Malbury tutted, "That name was not so difficult to give me. Who else?"

"There is no other name."

"I think you lie. And I think your partner Montjoy will be vastly more forthcoming when he has you as his evidence of failure to comply."

Titterstone's laugh was high-pitched, revealing stretched nerves even though he remained obstinate. "You won't shoot me. What would be the point?"

"Exactly. Failing the production of the file, tell me the name of your client."

"I cannot do that. I will not." The shadow disappeared as his arm dropped. His hand flattened on the blotter, fingertips nearly touching the discarded letter knife. "I cannot, not even for Boss Malbury's nephew. Whatever information you hope to gain, it will not ingratiate you with him. He won't find any loose ends knotted, only more dangling."

"We're talking about you and this file and your client. My patience is thin, three years thin. I shall inform my uncle that your divided loyalties forced my hand."

"Divided loyalties? Forced? No, sir. No!" His voice ratcheted up. "You cannot shoot me and escape. Think, sir! You are already in trouble with White Hall. Do you wish to run afoul of London's constabulary? Fire that pistol, and the watchmen will come."

"My uncle paid them to be elsewhere tonight. There's not a rat in London who would dare come on this street. The file, Titterstone. One last chance. That file or your client's name."

"You won't get away with this!"

The pistol cracked, sharp in the enclosed office.

Chapter 3

When the pistol cracked, Conrad clapped his hand over her mouth. Again. The sharp report of the pistol pierced the roiling bubble of fear and anger, terrified ice chilling her fire.

In the devastating silence, Phinney dragged away his sweaty hand and prayed—prayed! that Richard Malbury didn't search the closet for the file that Mr. Titterstone had refused to give him.

For he searched now. He opened drawers, cursed then slammed each shut before jerking open the next. When he stopped, several thumps sounded before he stomped away. Through that slender crack, she saw him pawing through a file from the shelving. He dropped it and reached for another from the neat stacks.

Conrad tried to pull her away from the door. Phinney dug in her heels and dug a warning elbow into his ribs. She refused to be a cornered cat. Here, she could make some attempt to fight.

Malbury hadn't re-loaded his pistol. Did he have another tucked into a pocket?

Conrad's cheek brushed hers. "Phinney," he whispered, "it's not safe."

She tightened her grip on his hand to let him know she understood their peril. Richard Malbury! After all these years. A murderer. He hadn't hesitated to shoot. Unless she counted all those pressing demands that Mr. Titterstone hadn't believed would lead to his death.

"Phinney, I want you behind me."

She dug in her fingernails.

He hissed. "Cat!"

The search in the office had stopped. Had Richard heard them?

"Mr. Titterstone?"

That was Mr. Gregory's gravel. The caretaker was walking into trouble. Her grip tightened on Conrad's hand.

"Sir? My apologies for disturbing you, sir. I heard a gunshot." The older man's voice sounded muffled, as if he remained in the outer office with a closed door. "I was down below, sir. The shot sounded as if it were in the building."

A rustle of paper, then steps hastened to the door.

"Sir. Where's Mr.—?" A plopping thunk, then a cry, followed by running feet, rapidly departing.

"Stay here," Conrad whispered.

"He'll hurt Mr. Gregory!"

"Hush! Stay out of sight! I'd rather no one knew that you witnessed anything, Phinney!"

"Yes, I'll stay."

Only then did he pull the door wide. His broad shoulders blocked her view of the room, then she saw the scattered papers, the ledgers and files on the floor—and Mr. Titterstone on the floor.

His eyes stared blankly. A hole centered his forehead with its receding hairline. Blood pooled under his head.

That blood would have to be scrubbed away before it stained the floor.

At that stupid thought, she shrank back into the closet. Nausea welled up. She pressed a hand to her mouth and swallowed and prayed it would pass.

Then she heard voices, Conrad's, smooth, over the gravel of the caretaker's. "Not hurt? Excellent. I need your help."

"But what happened, Mr. Hopson? Who wuz that man?"

"We'll need constables to work that out. And I'm Mr. Hoppock, Gregory. Constable Hoppock."

"Zounds, sir, I never. Why wuz ya clarking for Mr. Titterstone and Mr. Montjoy?"

"Gathering evidence. You need to find constables to help me, Gregory, and you may have to go far afield to do it. And tell Mrs. Gregory to expect them—and to stay off this floor."

"Right you are, sir. There wuz a new cleaning maid. She's to work this floor. She weren't below at her other work."

"If I see her, I'll intercept her."

"I could stay for you, sir, whilst you find your fellow constables and whatnot."

"I must preserve this crime scene, Gregory. I thank you for your service. My chief constable will also wish to speak with you. Go quickly, Gregory."

"Quick as this bum leg will take me, sir." Hobbling steps crossed the floor. A door was shut firmly, then fainter steps came back to the inner office and approached the closet.

Eying the door, Phinney backed into the blacker shadows.

Once again the door swung wide into the room. Conrad appeared, tall, blocky, his face shadowed, for the candle flickered behind him. "Come out here, Phinney."

She tried hard not to look at Mr. Titterstone. Conrad stood between them. Lifting the candle, he gestured for her to precede him to the outer office, a direction she was eager to take. He stepped back only to shut the closet door then joined her in the anteroom. He guided her to one of the straight-back chairs reserved for visitors to the firm.

Phinney sat before her shaky knees gave out. Reaction was taking over, just as it had when each of her parents died and when she received news of her sister Rosie's death. Strong in the actual moment, her body acted like water once the crisis passed.

She dragged off the mobcap and stared at the ruffled edge. A thread peeked from the edge. She tugged it, hoping Conrad wouldn't see her trembling.

He wouldn't tease her, not with a dead man mere feet away. Even the callow plowboy who had ribbed her mercilessly had never crossed that line. He wouldn't now, not when they had witnessed murder while a paneled door ensured their safety.

He crouched before her. "Phinney—."

She said the first fool thing on her tongue. "*Constable* Hoppock? You?"

His mouth twisted, and he edged back a few inches, as if he thought her question was evidence of her affront. "Yes."

"I thought you left to join the Bow Street Runners."

"I was convinced to get experience as a constable first."

"I trust you informed them of your past history of pranks and troubles."

He frowned. More inches came between them although his hand continued to rest on the chair arm. "They know what matters." He braced his other hand on the chair seat, bracketing her. "I want you gone from here before the other constables arrive. When my chief comes, I'll find out what questions he might want answered and put them to you myself. I don't want him to interrogate you."

She shuddered. "I doubt his interrogation would have the same end as Mr. Malbury's did."

Conrad glanced at the inner door. "No."

When he looked back, his hand shifted inward, and she felt its heat through layers of skirt and petticoats. The gentle pressure, human contact, friendly contact, stilled her trembling. The touch broke all social rules of etiquette. In the past, she would have railed at him. Now, she didn't care. Murder cast etiquette into the realm of inanity. In this moment, with Mr. Titterstone's eyes boring into her memory, she desperately needed his support.

"Go back to your home," he advised. "I know you want to forget this past half-hour, but I would rather you remember it. Remember everything they talked about. Remember exactly what you saw from the closet."

"I can write it down."

"Would you? That would help. Where can I find you? I'll come to you tomorrow, after noon."

"The Stowbridge Mission for Veterans Disabled in Portugal and Spain." When she gave the address, his eyebrows raised.

He didn't comment. He didn't ask the reason she lived at a mission. He didn't point out that the Stowbridge Mission was solidly in an impoverished neighborhood, not quite the East End but definitely sliding to join it. "You're safe there?"

"As safe as anyone can be in London."

"The children are with you?"

"Snug in their beds."

"Phinney—. I don't know how you came to London or why, but I'd rather you stay close in until we arrest this Richard Malbury."

"He didn't see me, Conrad. He has no reason to connect me with this office."

"He saw Gregory, and Gregory will gossip about the maid cleaning the upper floors. Then he'll have your name and your direction. No, you stay close in. Don't wander the streets. Don't come back here. As soon as I can, I'll move you and the two children."

"Three children."

"Three? I thought you said your sister had had two children."

"She did."

"Then the third—." He stopped.

Phinney guessed at the thought skittering through his brain—that the third child was hers. Her child when she was unmarried. The contraction of his brow added his next thought, that her departure from their home village of Brize Norton was driven by a fall from grace.

Phinney hadn't fallen for any man's line, and Vic was far from her child, but she didn't explain. Now wasn't the time, not when blood seeped into the floor of the inner office. Her story of leaving Brize Norton and then leaving Merrybush would take much more than a few minutes. Her acquisition of a boy from the streets of Liverpool would take many more minutes. And then she must explain her real reason for being in London, too many more minutes, especially since Conrad obviously wanted her to vanish before any other constables arrived.

"You'll have to give up this job, Phinney. I can support you until you find other employment. You *and* the children."

Her heart warmed at that addition. He was the Conrad she remembered, not jaded by his years dealing with the worst of London. "That isn't necessary, Conrad."

"I think it very necessary." He straightened, looming over her. "You need to keep safe."

"Because I am your sole witness." Glad her knees had lost their watery shakes, she stood. He didn't back up, so she let the chair scrape back, jamming into the wall in order to keep a few inches between them.

"Because I want you kept safe."

Surprised, she glanced up. "I want you safe, too, Conrad. You will take no risks."

"Yes, Josephine Elizabeth Darracott."

She didn't believe his meek acquiescence, but without any emotional hold on him, she could not demand. "I'm Mrs. Coates to the Gregorys. A widow. Recently from Shropshire. Remember that, Conrad."

"That sounds like a long story to me."

"You can hear it tomorrow—as well as learn the truth. And now, I had better leave." That was a lie, for she didn't intend to abandon her job, not when she would need to return for the file that Mr. Titterstone had hidden. The master key that opened all the offices remained in her pocket. Once she had that file, she would return the key to Mrs. Gregory—and never come back here again.

She wouldn't leave her employment before then, no matter what Conrad demanded. She had no power to dictate to him, and he had none over her.

"You'll be safe going home?"

"Of course. I know the route home, even in this fog. I've walked it many times," which was another lie, for she'd been employed only two days. "Oh, wait. My cleaning basket. I will need that."

"Where is it?"

She glanced back at the inner office, reluctant to enter the room and encounter those staring eyes.

"I'll fetch it."

He had no qualms, just entered and began a quick scan for the basket with rags and duster.

How many constables would come? How long would they stay?

At least one would inform the other clerks who worked for Titterstone and Montjoy. They would explain about the murder of the chief partner and then question them about Richard Malbury, a mysterious file, and Peter DeChambeaux, not forgotten though he and his wife had died two years previously. That constable would also question Mr. Bannockburn as soon as he arrived, a half-hour before the clerks began arriving. The middle-aged man opened the ground floor offices in preparation for the arrival of all the clerks, ensured that the Gregorys had stoked the furnace and cleared the hallways before stationing himself to greet the solicitors and barristers who filled the offices in the upper floors.. She had never seen him greet those men, but she had no doubt he would bow and scrape just like Mr. Peabody, the bald-pated chief clerk who had assisted the bishop in charge of the diocese of which Brize Norton was a small part.

Another constable would be sent posthaste to Mr. Montjoy's residence. Although that visit might be presumed as protection, a bright man would question the other lawyer about Malbury and files and a man two years dead. How would Mr. Montjoy greet the news of his partner's death? When she'd first seen the lawyers, at Parton March, she'd thought them an odd partnership. Rough Titterstone and suave Montjoy, the former incisive and the other creamily smooth. Equal partners who represented such men as the wealthy Bennett Howell Parton as well as the criminal Boss Malbury.

A third would inform Mrs. Titterstone of her husband's death. Would she know anything of his business affairs? Or was she like so many women, caught up in children and the household?

Phinney waited for Conrad and set her own plans. She had a good idea where Titterstone had hidden that file from Liverpool, the one that mentioned her late brother-in-law Peter DeChambeaux. Did it mention the unnamed client? Files about Richard Malbury and his uncle did not interest her—although the London constabulary would give them a very close read. How long would the constables remain, working through their investigation? Would they remain through tomorrow night? If they did, she would go about her work as usual, cleaning the third floor and then the fourth. She would come back again and again until she had two spare minutes alone in Titterstone's office. That's all the time she would need.

"You've gone into a brown study, Phinney."

She gave an involuntary start then a deliberate shake, as if casting off bad thoughts. Conrad handed her basket over. "My apologies. I will leave now. Mrs. Gregory must be expecting me."

Hurrying down the hall, she looked back once she reached the door that opened to the narrow back stairs.

Conrad had shut the office door.

She looked forward to the battle that his interrogation would be, him wanting information and her carefully parsing it out, him wanting her to leave her employment and her oh so carefully letting him think that she had.

. ~ . ~ . ~ .

Conrad stared at the ledgers on the floor. One had opened, revealing neat handwriting as it ticked off numbers. Then he scanned the shelves with few remaining stacks of files.

Richard Malbury had left a mess.

He had located Phinney's cleaning basket at the base of the shelving. Malbury must have seen it. Would he assume that she had left the basket behind when she finished her work? Or would he guess that the cleaning maid had hidden when he and Titterstone came in? Would he work out that she had hidden in the closet?

Would Malbury realize that she had heard everything that was said? Names. Information. Accusations.

And the murder.

How long before Malbury came looking for the cleaning maid who could identify him and give testimony naming him the murderer of George Titterstone?

Chapter 4

Vic held the lantern while Elise searched another box of papers. "Be sunrise before we're through," he warned. They couldn't see outside; the shutters blocked light both ways. No watchman could see their searching; they couldn't see the onset of day. "If your aunt finds us gone, she'll scream like a banshee."

"One more box, then we'll go. It's here, though. I know it's here." She shoved papers back into a file then piled all the files she had removed back into a box and closed the lid.

Propped against the outer door, Vic wished he could join her search, but he could barely string letters into words. Elise had only started teaching his letters when they were at Parton March. She could glance at a document and know if it had names that she knew. That's how she'd found the file while he unlocked that desk in Liverpool for Joe and Button.

The file she'd taken had her father's name and a London street address. He figured that address would be their next search.

Beyond that, Elise hadn't shared what she looked for. He did know that she wanted to know who caused her parents' deaths.

She tugged on the bottom box wedged into a corner. "Vic, help me."

He stepped over the boxes already searched, now scattered around her. Any order had got lost in her eagerness to get to the one beneath and the next one and the next.

The wooden crate was tucked between a larger crate and an exposed beam. He tugged and pushed, but it wouldn't shift. He shoved his shoulder into the crate and got a half-inch, less. "What's in this crate?"

"I don't know. The lid is nailed down."

"We need a crowbar."

"The watchman would hear that."

A screech of nails in wood would fetch trouble. Vic planted his feet and used his whole body for the next shove. Wood scraped over wood.

"Hsst! He'll hear!"

He worked into the narrow space, dropped enough to get his weight below the crate's center mass, then worked his feet up the wall before giving another shove. He got several inches, another loud scrape, a few squeals of iron, and Elise's slap on his arm.

"Stop it, Vic! We'll have watchmen up here."

He grabbed the wooden box. It moved easily. He lifted it out and onto a searched box, its lid askew.

She pounced before he was out of the way. He had to sidestep to get back to the door. Then he planted his ear against the wood.

That loud scrape worried him. The watchmen were alert, too alert for a building that looked abandoned and had rusty locks barring the back door. As Elise started her methodical search by the light of the shuttered lantern, he eased open the door to listen for investigating footsteps.

"Shut the door," she hissed. "The light."

He obeyed but fished out his picks and inserted them in the keyhole.

"Vic?"

The picks would block a key inserted from the other side. He backed away from the door.

Elise had the sense to shutter the lantern.

He strained to hear another soft sound like the first, the faintest creak of a step on the old stairway, the soft slide of a boot along the planks of the upper walkway with the half-dozen offices overlooking the main floor.

"Vic?" she breathed beside him.

"Ssss." The barest sound, not even a hiss. He backed into a box and sat quickly.

They were trapped here. The office had a window, but it was the height of three men off the floor. He didn't see a way to climb to the rafters.

Lamplight gleamed under the door. A boot slid across wood. The doorknob rattled as someone tried it.

He wished he could see his picks.

The soft footsteps moved on. The lamplight faded.

Vic waited then heard another doorknob tried. He crept back to the door, dropped to his knees, and tried to see through that half-inch crack beneath the door.

The warehouse ceiling was in darkness. Lamplight flashed on metal then moved on, unable to penetrate the cavernous open space.

More doorknobs rattled. Two then three more in steady succession. The watchman was heading back to this office and beyond the stairway that centered the upper balcony.

The light brightened again. Vic got an eyeful of two feet in leather. The knob rattled, then the watchman walked on. He pressed his hands flat then levered up, silent as a moth.

"Anything?" a man asked, his voice muffled.

"Nay. All locked tight. How 'bout your side?"

"All locked, like usual."

"Sound was outside then."

"Right above my head," the first man countered. "I told you. And I saw a light."

"Couldn't have, not from below. `Sides, nothing gets past the locks."

"I'm gonna check the outside doors."

"What for? Can't get past that rusted lock on the back, and Jamey's sittin' at the front. You got spooked, that's what, when the Boss's man came today, asking if we'd seen anything more than the rats."

Steps faded away, the stairs creaking as the two watchmen descended.

"Are they gone? Can I open my lantern?"

"Wait," Vic told her. He struggled out of his jacket, tighter fitting since he ate regular, ever since they'd left Liverpool. He stuffed the thin wool along the crack beneath the door. Climbing up, he withdrew his picks, listened, then gave Elise the word she needed. "Safe."

She unshuttered the lantern. Vic winced at the brighter light.

Elise reached into the box with more eagerness than she had earlier. Her mouth quirked to one side, the way it did when she got to an interesting part of a story. She opened a file. "Yes!"

"Sssss," he warned although she had whispered. "You found somethin'? Some*thing*," he corrected.

She ran one of her fairy fingers down the document, started to turn the page, then snapped the file shut. She set it on the floor and picked up another file. "I think. Maybe. Titterstone and Montjoy joined in a case with my papa."

He remembered the lawyers from Parton March, the skinny one who always smiled, the mustached man who had hired Stevens. He remembered Button's hand, falling from under the blanket that served as his shroud.

In the weeks since they left Liverpool and stayed at Parton March, he'd learned the Coates family weren't actually the Coates. Mrs. Coates wasn't the mother of Elise and Hank; she was their aunt. Their parents were killed, two years before, in a carriage accident. In the months after their deaths, the family house was burgled several times then burnt to the ground. They had stayed with friends until that house was burgled. Phinney had packed their few possessions and hustled them to another friend in a different village—only to have the burglary occur once again. She had then hauled him to Liverpool, the town where their parents died, the town where their father had had his law practice. But his office was closed, all the documents removed, the furniture sold for unpaid rent.

Vic met them when their money had run low and the children were thieving to fill their bellies. He hadn't wanted Elise and Hank to run afoul of the Liverpool gangs, so he taught them what he knew. Lonely himself, he accepted their offer of a roof.

Then came a press gang and the mustached man and his hired killer Stevens and their own flight from Liverpool, first to Parton March. There Vic spotted the mustached man and learned his name was George Titterstone. And from there Phinney decided answers to the deaths of her sister and brother-in-law might be found in London.

So here they were, Phinney off on her own search, and Elise determined to search as well, in a direction she hadn't shared with her aunt.

Her refusal to share information with her aunt worried Vic. They were children. Elise was barely ten. The watchmen who'd come looking were big men, braw with muscle. They would punch and kick long before they asked a question.

Elise added a second file to the first. Minutes later, a third and a fourth. Vic kept an ear to the door and hoped the watchmen wouldn't return. When he heard her shoving files back into the box, he turned. "Good. We can leave."

She had piled several files between her feet, more than the four he'd seen her stack.. "I want to look over these. Maybe Aunt Phinney will look over them with me. We should leave everything the way it was." She struggled to lift the box.

"We need to leave. We'll lock the door back. They'll never know we were here."

She didn't argue. She clasped the files against her chest, her arms wrapped protectively over them.

Vic's wish didn't come to fruition. They locked the door fine, but their last steps on the stairs were spotted. The man lifted a hullaballoo to call his fellow watchmen.

He jumped the last steps. Large thread bobbins were propped against a crate. He grabbed one and flung it at the watchmen. Another bobbin flew after the first. Grabbing a third, he scanned the nearby crates, looking for a target to cause the chaos that would aid their escape.

The third bobbin hit the watchman's shins. He swore roundly. "Jamey! Mac! Get yer arses over here! We got thieves!"

The shout echoed off the cavernous ceiling. His answer came back, and light brightened at the warehouse's front entrance.

"Little rats! I'll get ya." The man spread his arms wide to block the aisle. He plowed toward them. Pounding feet told help was approaching.

Vic found his chaos, a large crate with its lid pried off, packing straw sticking out. Colored jars lay on the straw. Four sat in a row before the crate.

He flung the lantern, light guttering as the arc of the throw threatened to douse the flame.

The lantern landed in the crate. The straw snatched the fire. Flames wooshed up.

"Water! Get water! We gotta fire!"

Vic ran for the back of the warehouse. Elise stayed on his heels. Behind them, the fire roared through the straw. Men shouted. He heard scraping and looked back. Two men strained to push the crate into the wide aisle, getting the fire away from the other crates. Another man hurried up with a bucket, water sloshing onto the floor.

"Vic!" Elise cried. "I can't believe you did that. What if the whole warehouse burns down?"

He hurried her out the door then shut it quick. He dug into his pocket for the rusted lock and snapped it back into place over the ring hasp. "You got your files."

"There may be more evidence. I thought we'd come back tomorrow—."

"Not if they don't stop that fire." Pleased with their escape, he jogged along the quay, heading for the alley to the street.

. ~ . ~ . ~ .

No one lurked on the backstairs as Phinney crept down. Mr. Gregory had vanished, off to fetch constables, as Conrad had ordered. Last night, the airless stairway hadn't worried her, and a high window on the attic level admitted the only light. Tonight, though, with rising fog obscuring the moon and stars, not even the faint light from streetlamps penetrated the stairwell's darkness. With murder fresh and the eyes of Mr. Titterstone haunting her, she hesitated on each landing. She strained to hear a scrape of a shoe or a heavy breath or the susurration of cloth, any sign that Richard Malbury hadn't fled the office building.

She clutched at the memory of Conrad, solid and assured, as ever he'd been. Nine years since their last meeting, he had surprised her. Taller, broader, his sturdy body well-formed even when he was no more than a plowboy for Squire Costell. He still planted his feet as if he stood on rich brown clods of dirt, though now he patrolled London's streets as a constable. He had braced her against him, and her trembling fear had eased.

With that memory bolstering her, she reached the ground-floor landing, with its narrow door leading to the steep, narrow steps to the cellars. The iron latch felt cold as ice. Fear again clutched her throat. After several swallows, she pushed it down and plunged into the darkness. She braced one hand on the dank brick wall, the other stretched before her, and took the stair step by step, slowly, carefully, fearfully. When her fingertips touched wood, she fumbled for the door latch and opened it to the warm light of the kitchen

A fire burned in the little hearth. It cast light and warmth into the wide room. Uncurtained half-windows revealed darkness in the back garden. Her sleeves rolled to her dimpled elbows and her apron strings tied in a drooping bow, Mrs. Gregory bent over a soapy basin in the dry sink. She scraped at a tin pot, muttering to herself about 'simple soaking'. The old mantel clock ticked on the side cupboard, its short pendulum counting off the seconds.

Phinney needed to leave, before the children woke and missed her. Their nightmares had ceased, thank God, during those long months in Liverpool, but occasionally they woke. They no longer screamed and cried about fire and death, but they lay stiffly, their eyes unblinking, their breaths rushed, until they would climb from their pallet and seek her side, tucking against her, wordless, cold, trembling. Since she'd begun this work, she thought Hank must seek out Elise, but her niece would not seek comfort. She would endure, shedding silent tears that stained her cheeks. Old beyond her years, Elise broke Phinney's heart. More than anything, she wanted to restore childhood to her niece and nephew.

And to Vic.

The boy was a godsend, not just in Liverpool when he kept them from starving and from falling into the clutches of the local gangs, but in distracting Elise and Hank from the difference between their former lives and their current one.

The boy broke Phinney's soft heart. He had a willingness to learn to read and cipher that spoke of an unexpressed ambition to improve himself. Although he was half her age, he gave them more protection on Liverpool's streets than she could offer the children, so she opened their meager one-room home to him.

Elise and Hank had dragged him home with a story of how he had saved them from a greengrocer. Phinney had worried that Vic was a petty thief there to steal what little they had. His speech was rough, his habits rougher. He knew the waterfront streets and gangs to avoid. No adult cared for him, and the only adult he mentioned had died several years previously. With wrists and ankles showing in too-small tattered clothes and boots starting to wear a hole on the side and in the sole, Vic looked like trouble. Her worries dissipated as he slowly revealed a good heart and strong loyalty and wariness determined to keep them all safe.

She had stood silent, caught by memory, much too long. Mrs. Gregory glanced over her shoulder. "What you standing there for, Mrs. Coates?"

Remembering Chessie, the dramatic upstairs maid at her previous position, Phinney clutched her hands to her bosom and heaved a sigh. "Oh, Mrs. Gregory, there's been murder done." For effect, she slumped against the door jamb. "It's quite sucked the strength from me." That wasn't too far from a lie.

"M'husband did tell me that he'd been sent to find a constable. He said there was a shot fired in an office on the fourth floor."

"Did you not hear the gunshot? I did, and I was on the third floor. I was just finishing my last job, polishing the door knobs all shiny for morning." The lie came pat, unplanned yet welcome. "I ran upstairs to see what happened, and the clerk there, he told me that one of the lawyers was dead. Shot dead, Mrs. Gregory."

"Awful it is. Did the clerk say who it was?"

"Mr. Titterstone. Murdered!" she added in a thrilling accent worthy of grease paint and the boards. Phinney tottered forward and pretended to fall into a chair beside the table. "I very nearly saw the murderer."

"What's this? What's this?" Mrs. Gregory wiped her hands on a dingy cloth. As she turned, she rolled down her sleeves, and Phinney realized that the older woman wasn't in her habitual chambray but wore mourning black. "Did you see someone on the back stairs just now?"

"No. Earlier. On the front stairs." She waved a hand before her face, as if she needed cooling. "When I heard the shot, I was that close to them that I nearly took those steps. Then I heard someone coming down and hied me back into an office and shut the door. I didn't want to see any murderer." She shuddered. "That murderer took the front stairs. Bold as brass," she added one of Chessie's favorite declarations.

"Will didn't say nothing about you being round when he was in that office, just told of a constable. He couldn't look much. The constable ordered him off to alert others. You say you saw a clerk?"

Phinney gave a great nod. "Yes. I recognized him." She made no mention of her previous acquaintance with Conrad Hoppock. Nor of one summer in Brize Norton, before her father died, when Richard Malbury came to visit his friend James Costell and lorded around the village, attempting to tumble anything in dimity skirts. "That clerk has worked late before. Mr. Gregory said he was a constable?"

"He did, indeed, but little more than that. Well," she lowered her bulk onto another chair and propped her elbows on the table. "This is a fine kettle of fish. Mr. Titterstone dead and a clerk who's a constable."

"What if he comes back?" she whispered.

"Who?"

"The murderer? What if he comes back and kills us all?"

"He won't be coming back tonight, not with constables coming."

"But tomorrow night? Or the next? We'll be so busy working—. We'd never know if he crept up behind us."

"Hush now. There's no need to worry. He'd be a fool indeed to come back here." She patted Phinney's knee. "You're safe, Mrs. Coates. The constables will be here as soon as Will fetches them back. They'll find the man what killed poor Mr. Titterstone. And he'll soon find himself with a rope on the gallows."

She shivered but nodded obediently, as if Mrs. Gregory had reassured her. She didn't want to play up her fear too much, for Mrs. Gregory might say that Phinney need not come back for a couple of days. The woman wouldn't do that, though. She wouldn't want to clean the four floors of offices by herself. And Phinney wouldn't let her make the offer, for she needed to come back for that file from Liverpool.

The memory of Elise's description of that night, of the two ruffians who had hired Vic, now dead because they knew who had hired them to steal the file from that office. Or were they dead because Elise had also taken a file? A file with her father's name, Peter DeChambeaux. Just as Peter's name was mentioned tonight by Titterstone, a dead man who could not possibly interest Richard Malbury or his uncle, the infamous Boss Malbury. A name in a file.

Had her brother-in-law's name caused the murders, first in Liverpool and here in London tonight?

Why would the name of Peter DeChambeaux be dangerous?

"Mrs. Coates?"

She started then shivered, blinking rapidly as if to stave off tears. "My apologies, Mrs. Gregory. I was—remembering."

"Did you see or hear aught to remember?"

"Nothing before. I was finishing my work. But when I went upstairs and was talking to the clerk, the one that's a constable, I looked into Mr. Titterstone's office, and I … saw … him."

"Poor thing." Her knee was patted once more. "I was just going to put on the kettle. Would you like a cuppa, Mrs. Coates? I missed mine because I came late. I was off to see a friend."

"Mr. Gregory mentioned that you would be late. He asked me to clean the front landings. I swept and dusted for you before I started my work."

The middle-aged woman levered her bulk up. She fetched the kettle from its hook by the fire and carried it to the dry sink where she had a water pitcher. "I was visiting a friend what lost her husband yesterday. An accident on the docks. I thank you for doing that bit of work for me." She carried the kettle back to its hook and swung it over the fire. "We'll have hot tea in just a mite."

"I'll have to scrub Mr. Titterstone's blood."

The woman gave a start. She grabbed her apron and twisted it. After long seconds, she released the fabric and smoothed it down. Without looking at Phinney, she took cups and saucers from the cupboard and brought them back to the table. "Don't you be worrying about that tonight. Like as not, those constables won't let the office open in the morning." She glanced at the clock and amended, "In just a few hours. Mr. Titterstone's office probably won't open for several days. Out of respect for the poor man. Poor Mr. Montjoy, losing his business partner. Whatever will he do? Mr. Titterstone saw to the bulk of their clients. Mark my words, that murderer is one of Mr. Titterstone's clients. He sees the rough ones and finds them a good barrister. Some of them get off, too, no matter what the Crown claims they done. I don't see how he can help such men, seeing all they've dirtied their hands with."

Phinney scarce heard the woman. Tomorrow night and the next was enough time to search the office and discover the importance of that sole painting. Richard Malbury wouldn't return until he was certain the constables had finished and gone. "Have you any work for me, Mrs. Gregory? Look. My hands are still shaking." She exaggerated the shake, and the woman tutted. "I did finish all the other offices on my floors. I'd even swept and dusted the corridor. I can't just sit here, thinking about all that happened."

"Never you mind that, Mrs. Coates. Why, you're white as this cream." She set the pitcher beside the cups. "You've finished your work?"

"All that I can do. I wish I were home in my bed, with my wee ones tucked up with me."

"You go on home and come back tomorrow, just as usual."

"Leave before my time's in? What will Mr. Gregory say?"

"Like as not, he won't notice, and if he says aught, he'll have to listen to me."

"I can't leave, Mrs. Gregory. I don't dare shirk my duties. I don't want my pay docked. The children and I need those coins. But oh, if I could have their little arms around me, I know I wouldn't be so scared."

"He won't dare report you, not when I tell him you had finished your work and some of mine. He's not here to see how scared you are. I am. He'll have to listen to me."

"I'll be better tomorrow. I promise. It's just the—the shock. I keep seeing those eyes—!" Another dramatic shudder, worthy of the maid Chessie, requiring less acting for the shock and horror.

Mrs. Gregory helped Phinney with her cloak then followed her to the door that let onto the back garden and led to a narrow lane that wended behind the buildings before reaching a cross street. "It's so late, it's early. The sun may be coming up before you reach home. The fog's thick, though. Strange, this time of year. You hurry home, now, and I'll see you tomorrow night. Don't worry about my Will. I'll talk to him."

Mission accomplished, Phinney thanked the woman again.

Tomorrow night she would return and find the file Mr. Titterstone had denied to Richard Malbury. Tonight she would be early home rather than dragging in well after dawn. She would get Elise to show her that file from the Liverpool office. On her previous look through the file, she hadn't seen anything. After tonight, she would look much more closely. Drawing her hood over her hair, she made for the garden gate.

Chapter 5

Conrad braced a hand on the window's inner casing. Beyond his glassy reflection he saw very little of the street below or the building across. The obscuring fog hid all but a faint glow of the lamplight, like will o'the wisp over a bog. As a boy he'd pursued the golden globes of light over chancy ground that gave under his bare feet.

He'd told himself that Phinney wouldn't leave the building by the front door. He prayed she wouldn't. Yet here he was, watching for her, another elusive wisp of a wish, an old dream he should give up. That dream had driven him to close the gulf between them by attending the Dame School, burning precious candle stubs for his ciphers and borrowing old primers from Lawyer Avesbury. The old lawyer was the one who explained the opportunity for advancement offered by the Bow Street Runners.

The day he left for London, his last day in Brize Norton, Phinney was agog with news of the summer fête hosted by Squire and Lady Costell. Twice he tried to tell her that he was leaving. Each time someone interrupted. With a frown at Conrad, her father asked her to take a copy of his sermon to Miss Purdy, the spinster at Mill's Race. Then her friend Chloe came, bubbling with news that her sister had accepted William Avesbury's proposal.

When he convinced her to walk with him, he'd guided her to the lane where spent rose petals and dried leaves scattered over the ground. Birds fluttered, pecking at the rose hips and flitting into the tumbling rose hedges. When they reached the end of lane, opening onto the grassy fields with grazing cows, he knew he wouldn't tell her.

He stole a kiss, though. "Stop talking, Phinney."

Her brown eyes opened wide. "Whyever should I?"

He quickly pressed his mouth to hers. Her soft lips, the sweet warmth of her breath, the trembling of her body—those haunted him still. With birds chirping and bees droning, the warm sun in a blazing blue sky, and greeny pastures around them, that was the memory he clung to when he walked his beat on cold nights. When he dealt with the worst of London, that memory sustained him. He tried not to think of her when he hauled the dregs into gaol.

Never had he imagined her in London. She was always there at the end of the lane, with the sun gilding her brown hair, her wide eyes tempting him, a pert comment falling from her lips.

Yet here she was, cleaning offices for crooked attorneys, witness to a murder, and heading off for her home, all alone, because duty demanded he preserve the scene. He had known she'd left Brize Norton when her father died, but he had hoped she was at her late sister's home in Merrybush.

Why was she in London?

And how had she come by that third child?

No. Conrad pushed away from the window. Avoiding Titterstone's body, he walked around the desk and into the anteroom. He shut the door to the inner office but not on his clamoring thoughts. To silence them, he forced his thoughts away from Phinney and back to London, back to the casework that had placed him in this office, another night and another death.

Weeks and weeks ago, his partner MacBride had jimmied a lock while Conrad kept watch. The late hour ensured the neighbors were asleep. The past day's watching ensured that the servants had left the house. The owner lay in the morgue, fished out of the Thames downriver from the bridge. The two servants had abandoned the house in the early morning hours.

"Hsst," MacBride warned.

Conrad bounded up the steps as his fellow constable opened the door and slipped inside. They shook rain off their coats then walked into the cold kitchen. When he located a candle, MacBride struck a flint and gave them light.

"What're we looking for, anyway, Hoppock?"

"Maps. Anything in French. Anything that looks like a government document."

"Lead on, MacDuff."

Conrad opened the door to the hall and stopped. "You smell smoke?"

"Can't smell nothing. M'wife's decided we need a cat. Could be hearth fire still smoking. Wind could be blowing down a chimney."

He sniffed as he stepped into the hall. Then he saw golden light shafting across the hall from under a closed door. It shifted, leaped, an agitated light that gave false hope.

MacBride elbowed past him and lifted his candle high. "You see that? No one's supposed to be here. I didn't see any light when we came along the street, did you?" He didn't wait for an answer. "Take this." He shoved the candle at Conrad while his right hand dove into his coat and drew out a pistol.

"I don't think—."

"Follow me. We'll see who's here."

Conrad followed the older man, but he tugged on his coat before they reached the room. "It's a fire."

MacBride grunted. "In the very room we need." He grabbed the doorknob then snatched back his hand. "Demmed hot. Gimme a handkerchief."

When he turned the knob and opened the door, the fire roared delight. Flames gushed toward them.

Conrad leaped back. He jerked MacBride with him only because he hadn't released the man's coat. They stumbled and fell, and the fire followed. The flames grabbed the lintel of the door and greedily licked at the new fuel.

MacBride yowled and slapped at his face and his coat. Conrad scrambled up and hauled the man to his feet, shoving him toward the kitchen. He had one quick look at the fire-filled room. The flames reached for the higher ceiling of the hall.

The windows exploded before they reached the main street. Fire licked up the front façade, reaching for the first floor.

He settled the moaning MacBride then banged on the doors of the neighboring houses. Soon the street filled with people scurrying to stop the fire's spread to the other houses. Someone ran for the fire brigade, but it was the pelting rain that saved the neighbors. By dawn, the house was gutted, the fire-singed MacBride was borne to a nearby hospital, and Chief Constable Hector Evans stood beside Conrad as the last support beams fell into the charred ruins.

Evans scowled. He wiped at the raindrops dripping off his hat brim. "We've lost another link to the master spy."

"You think he did this?"

"He's killed before to protect his identity. Now Stephen Phillips is cold in the morgue, and his house is burnt before we can search it."

"We're running a trail without a scent then."

"Not quite. We've one more link. We'll get you in place next week. An oblique connection. That might slip past the mastermind's notice."

Conrad hadn't asked what the chief meant. The late Stephen Phillips, cold in the morgue, bore the actual name of Etienne Philippe Durant. His alias no longer would shield his undercover work for Napoleon. The trail left sticky traces from France to the firm of *Titterstone & Montjoy*. That was Chief Evans' oblique connection. Conrad guessed that one of the attorneys, maybe both, knew the identity of the French master spy, either because they participated in his nefarious work against the British government or because he held information over their heads that forced them to work with him.

What would Chief Evans say when he saw George Titterstone dead? This murder couldn't be blamed on the master spy. Richard Malbury pursued some twisted order from Boss Malbury who ruled London's underworld.

Then he remembered Titterstone's comment that Malbury had worked with French spies. He remembered that the executed Robert

LeBrun had named the young peer in his last-minute confession.

Had Malbury acted for his uncle?

Or was he taking orders from the French spymaster?

Pounding footsteps caught his attention.

Old Gregory couldn't move that fast—and he hadn't had time to find any constable bribed to be far away from his appointed rounds.

The steps became lighter as the person left the stairs and came rapidly along the hall.

Conrad didn't have his pistol. After Mr. Bannockburn's constant encroachment on his space, pointing out Conrad's copying mistakes, he hadn't dared carry it. *Titterstone & Montjoy, Solicitors* was the last link. Being unmasked as a constable would be a fiery explosion that destroyed the entire investigation.

He left the candle burning and planted himself behind the door.

The steps slowed and became cautious.

He braced.

The doorknob rattled then the door opened inward, effectively hiding Conrad.

The man came into the room. He swung the door lightly shut.

And Conrad sprang.

He grabbed the man's shoulder. His fist swung. The man blocked it and drove in with a punch aimed at his stomach. With his left hand, Conrad punched down the blow. His right forearm shoved into the man's chest. He staggered back. Conrad threw another punch. Then he saw the young man's face.

Timothy Gibbons grabbed the slowing fist and thrust it away. "Constable 'oppock! It's me!"

Tension leeched away. Conrad slapped the Cockney constable's shoulder. "You're here. Faster than I expected."

"The old man said you needed 'elp. He said 'murder's been done'. Who 'ave you killed?"

"Not me." He jerked his head toward the inner office. "Our suspect."

"Chief won't be 'appy."

"Nor am I."

"Did you see who did it? Why didn't you arrest 'im?"

"I will. As soon as I can."

"You let him escape?"

"I was protecting a witness." Then he wished he hadn't revealed that. The constabulary leaked like a sieve when big arrests were in the offing. For a distraction, he added, "The murderer bragged that he had bribed the local constables to be far away from their usual routes tonight."

The body in the inner office had snared Timothy Gibbons's

attention, but at the implied accusation his attention slewed back to Conrad. "Not me."

"Did someone approach you?"

"Aye. Last night. Your murderer an old man with silvered muttonchops? French accent?"

"Young. Clean-shaven." Hearing about the French accent elevated Conrad's hopes. Here would be another link to the master spy—and confirmation that Malbury answered to the French more than to his uncle, no matter what he'd told Titterstone.

"Young. No beard," Gibbons mused. "That may `ave been the man `anging back `alf a block."

"Could you identify him again?"

"Old man? Sure. Young man?" He shrugged his answer.

"What did he say?"

"That he would make it worth my while to enjoy myself at the Seven Bells' even-odd wheel. Only he called it *roulette.*"

A French name for the French wheel, not the black-white E.O. wheel used in most of the gaming hells. Conrad crossed his arms and looked down his nose at the younger constable. "How come you're not at the Seven Bells? Didn't you take his money?"

"I took it." Gibbons' wide grin celebrated the trick he'd pulled. "But duty calls. And the bribe meant trouble was afoot. I'll not miss that. Seems I missed the worst of it, though."

"Not quite. There will be more after tonight, and the chief will need to know who he can trust."

At the words, Gibbons' chest puffed out. Remembering his own first years on the force, Conrad hoped his next order didn't deflate the cub.

"Go to the chief. Tell him what's happened here—that murder's been done at this office."

"I'll tell him. No name?"

"Not yet. And Gibbons, watch the Cockney."

"Oh, aye. You staying here?" he added, careful with his H.

He thought of the ledgers and scattered papers. "I'll be searching for evidence." The evidence that Richard Malbury had wanted. A file.

What information was so important?

Would it convict Boss Malbury of a single percent of the crimes he'd ordered done?

Or offer proof of the French spymaster's identity? Documentation of his work against White Hall? Or a list of the people who worked for him? People like an old man with a mutton-chop beard and a French accent, even after years as an *émigré* in London.

Chapter 6

The gate creaked on its hinges when Phinney opened it wide. She slipped through and let the gate fall close, the hasp banging onto the loop.

As the night had cooled, fog had risen from the Thames and crept into streets and byways nearest the river. It touched her face with damp and cloying fingers, and she tugged her wool hood closer, hoping to leave the thickening vapor behind when she left the riverside.

Although lamps were lit at the street corners, the blanketing fog limited the light's reach, leaving pavements in darkness. Phinney walked rapidly. Over the past four nights of her work, she'd memorized her route by landmarks at the corners. She tried not to think of Mr. Titterstone's eyes and the blood pooling on the floor.

That Richard Malbury had turned into a murderer didn't surprise her. He'd had only one visit to Brize Norton, a summer six years ago. He hadn't impressed her then. He impressed the young Costell sisters and Susannah Wylie and Marianne Langley with descriptions of balls and parties and private clubs and riding in Hyde Park. He talked of his father's great estate just beyond Richmond and his mother's connections to the great names like the Eatons and Cowpers, the Westovers and Castlereaghs, and more.

Concerned with her father's declining health, Phinney knew her distracted responses to his sallies and compliments didn't please him. By their third meeting, Richard Malbury didn't seek her out for conversation.

Phinney hesitated at a corner. Her way took her into a narrow lane between two buildings, one a story taller than the other. She peered into the fog, yellowed by lamplight. Creaking wheels and the steady clipclop of hoofbeats warned of an approaching vehicle. She crossed the street and dodged into the lane before she saw the horse. As she walked along the lane, she kept close to the side of the bricked building, for it had no doorways that opened onto the lane.

Before that summer ended, her father died, plunging her into mourning. The flowers on his grave hadn't wilted before the parish bishop informed her that a new vicar was appointed. She had to vacate the vicarage for the man and his family.

Occupied by memories of her last summer in Brize Norton, she didn't listen for anyone else. No one walked the streets this late or this early, depending on one's bedtime. What had Shakespeare said? *It is so very late that it will be early by and by.* Something like that. She noodled over which play as she crossed from the lane and followed the street.

A hackney coach trundled over the cobbles. At the corner, Phinney had to wait for the coach to pass—and she heard the scrape of a boot heel on rock. The unusual sound in the usual quiet solitude startled her.

The horse plodded past. The coachman sat hunched over the reins, drowsing as he let the horse find the way back to the stable.

Phinney veered a little to cross behind the wheels. She hurried, skipping to step onto the pavement. A lamppost glowed ahead. The fog diffused its light. Even if she turned, she might see no one behind her.

But she listened.

There. Was that a footstep falling right after hers?

Am I being followed?

By whom? A footpad? Or Richard Malbury?

Why would he follow her? How would he know to follow her, a simple cleaning maid? How would—?

She stopped abruptly, for she saw again her basket with its rags and polishes, abandoned at the base of the shelves where Mr. Malbury had searched the files.

Her abrupt stop took the follower by surprise, for several footsteps sounded sharply before he stopped.

Phinney wanted to turn and confront the man, but—if it were Richard Malbury, he'd had time to reload his pistol.

No. Wait. Bullets and black powder were not easily carried. This summer a ton *vivant* would not want any bulky items to ruin the closely tailored line of his coat. She doubted Richard Malbury had changed that much in his exile.

She considered running. He couldn't shoot her in the back if he hadn't reloaded. But Richard would soon win any footrace. That long-ago summer, he had touted his athleticism to any who would listen, recounting bouts at Gentleman Jackson's club on Bond Street or mock duels at Angelo's Fencing Academy.

Ice froze her lungs. She had no doubt Richard Malbury followed her, a simple cleaning maid, whose disappearance would rouse no suspicions—especially not after Phinney's enactment of fear for Mrs. Gregory. Would he strangle her? Or bludgeon her to death? Would he toss her body into the Thames?

No. The river was too far. He would attract attention if he carried her body.

Or not, in this fog.

He would want to rid himself of a cleaning maid who had inconveniently heard his talk with Mr. Titterstone. And heard him shoot the lawyer.

He wouldn't know that Constable Conrad Hoppock had also heard both conversation and murder.

What am I to do?

The sharp crack of that gunshot that killed George Titterstone still pierced her ears. If she were Richard, she would have brought a second pistol and hidden it in her pockets or her reticule. She'd seen a small single-shot pistol. Richard had used a dueling pistol. Did he have one of the newer single-shots? Those pistols were not as accurate. Could she risk out-running him?

She resumed walking, maintaining her former pace as she reached the lamppost and continued on. Half up the block, she passed a doorway and risked a backward glance. The follower had reached the lamppost. The fog-diffused light gleamed on the man, slim. She could not gauge his height. He wore a light-colored suit with a reddish vest. A steeply-crowned hat with a deeply bent brim hid his face and hair.

She hurried, eagerly striding for the next lamppost. Her hood hid her own hair and features. Richard Malbury thought he pursued a cleaner. She didn't want him to discover that he knew the woman who could testify against him. Almost to the corner, she crossed, avoiding the glowing light of the lamppost.

The street was rising, working up with the land. She recognized the bow-fronted haberdasher. Beyond that shop were steps between the buildings, a close that climbed through pitchmirk. Pedestrians who took the steps would have shorter work of the rise to the next street. The steps, though, misdirected her a full block. If she didn't cut back to the right, she would lose her next street.

I can find it. I know my route in daylight. I won't miss it. All I must do is elude Richard Malbury until sunrise.

His footsteps sounded louder. She risked a glance and saw him angling toward her.

She reached the steps, dark and scary by day, terrifying this night.

Phinney darted into the close.

She tripped immediately, falling forward onto her hands. Her wrists and shoulders jarred from her weight. She cried out—then clamped her mouth shut. She pushed upright. Jerking her skirts high, she rushed upward, hoping the steps were equally spaced, hoping the stones didn't tilt under her feet.

"Don't run," drifted up the stairs. Malbury's voice. "I just want to talk."

She stumbled against the wall.

He laughed. "Stay there. We can talk. I've got a gold coin that says you need to hear what I say."

He thought he dealt with an ignorant girl, easy prey.

Phinney pushed off the wall and hurried on, stubbing her toes.

Lured by the square of brighter shadows at the top of the stairs, she fell forward. She caught herself on the wall. She couldn't hear him. Her breathing gusted, drowning other sounds. Her spine tingled, like fingers ran down her backbone. She shoved away from the brick and ran up the last steps.

She burst out of the close.

Lamplight across the way seemed bright after the utter darkness of the stair. Spurred by fear, she dashed across the street. She ran along the pavement, passing a lamppost and another and another and on to the next block with its own series of lamppost, until her lungs wanted to burst.

Phinney collapsed against the wood embrasure of a shop window. She tried desperately to breathe. Her palms stung. Her knee complained. Her shin burned. Tears filled her eyes. She wiped them away and peered into the fog.

That deep rumble was a heavy wagon rolling over the cobbles. The fog obscured the dray, but she heard the clipclop horse hooves, doubled. And footsteps, sharp, approaching.

The fog wafted slowly, blocking her view. Unable to see the wagon or the man who followed her, Phinney slid backwards, leaving the window, scraping over the façade, then the wall opened to a recessed door, and she fell in, catching herself against the door. A faint tinkle of a bell.

The wagon came closer. The footsteps ceased. She crammed into the corner.

The footsteps came on. The wagon's rumbling almost overwhelmed the footsteps, but the sharp thud of bootheels was distinct. Not running. Steady. Assured of success.

She clapped a hand over her mouth, trying to muffle her gasping breaths.

Dark shapes loomed in the fog. The horses. Slowly passing. Then the wagon, a heavy freight dray, laden with barrels.

And the footsteps, close but not as close as she would have expected, approaching, then receding, fainter and fainter, leaving.

She sagged against the doorway.

He wasn't gone. Richard Malbury wouldn't give up that easily. He was across the way, going along that side of the street as he looked for her. He had to rely on sound as well, and the heavy freight wagon had obscured her lighter steps, her shoes lacking the harder soles of his boots.

Phinney peeked out. The footsteps were totally obscured now. The wagon was lost in the fog although she could still hear it. She started after it, hastening, careful to keep her soft-soled shoes from making a sound. They were going in the same direction that Malbury would be.

Soon he would cross and come back in his search of her side of the street. She needed to be off this street, winding along one of the dozen little side byways. There she could lose him—and not lead him to the Stowbridge Mission.

And Peter DeChambeaux's two children.

She continued to follow the freight wagon, past three cross streets, until she happened upon an angled street that she recognized. Richard Malbury's footsteps were lost now. She hoped that meant she had lost him as well. The wagon continued on while she ventured onto the angled street. Fog and darkness cloaked her until she passed under the corner lampposts, but she was merely a woman in a dark cloak to anyone who saw her.

Other pedestrians trickled along the streets. Dawn was pressing close. Away from the river the fog had thinned a little. Lampposts and the occasional lighted windows offered hopeful golden glows. She no longer feared the streets she walked along. These were better shops, with homes tucked into corners and down meandering lanes. Her racing heart slowed. Her breath came evenly. She studied the few people that she passed. What if a man in a light-colored suit with a Paris beau-style hat loomed out of the fog? She didn't know. Her options for escape were more and more limited.

The angled street divided into two narrow byways. Lamplight revealed a shop front that she recognized, so she took the left-hand path and plunged into a rabbit's warren that she'd learned in the past week on visits to the market and a park. The rumbling carts were lighter, pushed by men. The footsteps were muffled or thumped. She passed more people. She recognized more shops. Her hurts demanded attention. She ignored them and kept walking, kept spotting the next landmark.

The narrow byways gave onto a lane which led to a wider street. The fog had lightened, for she could see the house roofs and pink in the clouds. A big man with a coat stretched tight over his back and heavy boots stomped out of an alley and crossed the street. Fog swallowed him before he reached the other side. On another lane on she followed a tall man with a flopping hat and a bulging pack, jingling and clanking like a country tinker. He kept to the street, moving over only for the pushcarts.

She turned a corner and came on two young women in grey skirts, knitted shawls tucked in their waistbands. Arm in arm, they walked slowly, tired after their night's work, cleaning maids for the many offices that blanketed the city. Their employers wanted the drudges out of sight of clients. Only clerks interacted with the elite, who never knew that dust settled on polished wood and dirt had to be scrubbed from entryways, carpets had to be beaten clean, and coal ash had to be collected and carried elsewhere.

Phinney winced at her bitter thoughts. Before her parents' deaths, she never considered the unseen work that eased her life. She knew the work of maids and gardeners and cooks, all seen but barely acknowledged. As a governess for the Kimbrel children, her station placed her lower than her employers and above the servants, fitting neither level. The servants knew she was better born and better educated than both Mr. and Mrs. Kimbrel, which layered yet another barrier between her and them.

Her work now ranked her as one of the unseen yet vital cleaners, much like the gruff man who had done the rough work at the vicarage. When she dealt with him, standing on a back step to give her orders, his gaze never lifted from the ground. The housekeeper had always paid him, as if Phinney's hands were too pristine to risk contact with his hands grubby from manual work. He was another of the hidden workers that she had never imagined until she became one of them. In Liverpool she'd taken in piecework, sewing and embroidery, and earned barely enough for them to subsist on. Vic's arrival had saved them from both starvation and the unconscious mistakes that had kept their neighbors hostile.

She felt akin to the workers she passed, the grizzled man with his pushcart, the skinny lad jogging into the fog, all of them heading for jobs that barely kept them clothed and fed and warm.

Daylight increased. More people milled about or walked steadily to their work. The difference between her and these other people now had starker lines than before. How many had seen murder done? How many had scurried ahead of a pursuit? How many had hidden from a dangerous criminal?

She glanced at the furrowed brow, sunken eyes, and tightly-compressed mouth of a passing woman.

More people than she had realized.

She passed homes with little porches only three steps above the street, more store fronts, cobbler and cutler, seamstress and tailor, services rather than merchandise.

At a corner stood a woman in an apron and knitted shawl. At her feet was a large basket, covered with a cloth. "Hot buns," she called. "Only a ha'penny." Her silver hair was in a neat bun at her nape. Her faded plaid skirt was patched but clean. A hard life had given her a narrow face, but her mouth wasn't pinched. Her eyes were clear of the Blue Ruin that infected some of the poor. Her baking showed industry rather than sloth. "Hot buns, hot buns. Fresh from the oven."

Phinney dug into her skirt pocket and found a clipped penny. "Good morrow."

Fingers knotted with arthritis took the penny and dropped it into a cup tucked into the basket. Parts of her nails were blackened, all of them ragged. After cleaning out ash in still-warm hearths, Phinney knew coal dust didn't easily scrub off.

The bun steamed when Phinney tore it open. "You must have risen early to bake these."

"I do it every morning. Sell most at building sites."

"Will you give me some directions? I lost my way in this fog."

"I can hear yer not from these parts."

"I was raised in a village called Brize Norton."

"Might should go back there. London's hard on young lasses like you."

Phinney smiled. "You sound like my granny. I'm here now. It will take more coins than I have to go back. I'm looking for Church Cottages Lane."

"Yer not that far off. If 'tweren't a fog, you could see the steeple. Just a few blocks over." She gave simple directions. When thanked, the woman shook her head. "If you can't go back, then you need to learn several paths to your home. Not everyone in London is a friend."

"I hope you sell all of your baking."

"I could sell more. Do you bake?"

"I wish."

"Learn." Then she lifted her call of "Hot buns" once more.

She followed the woman's directions to venture to the right at the next corner, go three blocks, then turn left and left. That street would lead to Church Cottages, the woman had said, and so it did. A mottled brick building rose to her left. She passed church steps that she recognized from last Sunday's service. An iron paling fence ran beside the cemetery then a brown brick building that housed the vicarage, then an opening blocked by green-painted gates.

She reached the corner, and the narrow street gave onto a wider one, with lampposts at each corner. Across the way was Stowbridge Mission, the fog cleared enough to offer the whole of the four-storied building. Unneeded lamplight shined on the steps and the porch.

As she stood at the corner, praying gratitude for coming safely home, she saw two urchins slip around the railing and up the steps to the double entry. The boy was all brown, hair and clothes and boots. The other's blonde hair gleamed brighter than the lamplight.

Elise. With Vic. No Hank, which was one relief.

But those two would know her wrath for leaving the mission's safety.

Chapter 7

When Chief Constable Hector Evans narrowed his lichen green eyes, Conrad cringed inwardly, anticipating the questions to come.

"Sir Roger Nazenby will be disappointed. He expected George Titterstone to lead us to the ring of French spies who have eluded us for a decade."

He rested his hand briefly over the dead man's eyes, a gesture that heartened Conrad. In this job, one danger was becoming calloused, for the Constabulary saw the worst that humans did to each other.

The chief rose and stepped around the desk. He stared at the ledgers and files scattered over the floor. "Are you certain that the man who shot him is Richard Malbury?"

"Titterstone called him by that name. Malbury said that he gave this firm charge of his affairs when he fled abroad. Now that the elder Malbury's health is declining, his son wants to return home and live on the fringes of society, the way his uncle Boss Malbury does."

"His uncle Boss Malbury? That's a relation the lord has previously denied. I'm not certain Nazenby has acted on that connection of nobility to the London criminals. Nor has his second in command, Lord Giles Hargreaves." He bent, retrieved one of the ledgers and thumbed through it. "They linked the Honorable Richard Malbury to the French spies—but not the boss and certainly not Lord Malbury. Well, well, well. We needed hard evidence for an arrest. The son of a peer of England has more protections than I like, and his father enlisted his friends to block our investigation. Nazenby wasn't pleased at the delay."

"So Malbury escaped." Finally, he had an answer to one puzzle. As for the second—. "Sir, I thought the spy ring collapsed."

"One of the rings. The one that worked exclusively in the *haut ton*. The other had fingers in several levels of society: the *ton*, city aldermen and financial leaders, the criminal underworld. We never found the mastermind of that ring."

"And the evidence against Richard Malbury? What was the problem? I know he was named in the confession of that executed spy Robert LeBrun."

"Lord Malbury had a—let's call him a friend—situated on the cabinet, a special adviser to an important minister. He questioned if a coerced confession should hold any weight. We didn't stop investigating, but the question blocked Nazenby's order of arrest for several days." Evans closed the ledger with a snap then placed it on the corner of the desk. He toed another ledger but didn't pick it up. "By the time Nazenby removed the impediment to his arrest, LeBrun was hanged and Malbury on the Continent. We lost track of him after Belgium."

"I remember the name Claude Thierry. He's in prison, isn't he?"

"In prison awaiting trial, with influential friends visiting weekly and Nazenby's petition to move for a secret trial also blocked. Thierry was arrested several months with LeBrun, but he remains in prison while LeBrun hanged for spying. Malbury wasn't named specifically in LeBrun's confession. With the second spy ring still operating, Hargreaves refuses to allow his wife to testify in open court. He doesn't want her targeted for a second time by the spies. Nazenby's petition for the secret trial might be approved if we could connect Thierry to this second spy ring. We know his orders came from someone in London. He had no direct contact with France, not after the death of Celeste Sourantine, who served as their courier to France."

"All depends on locating the leader of this second spy ring."

Evans picked up a second ledger, flipped it open and scanned the contents before placing it with the first one. "We need an auditor to run through these ledgers and the files."

"You think Titterstone would commit anything to paper? Especially anything that connected him to Boss Malbury or to this French mastermind?"

"Attorneys write things down. Part of their collection of evidence. I would like to know what Titterstone knew—and how much his partner Montjoy knows. How much of Titterstone's conversation with Malbury did you hear?"

"Everything that happened in this room." He gestured to the closet, its door partially open. "I hid there." He found himself reluctant to mention Phinney. Yet he should share the information with his chief. Secrets always came back to bite. "I was hiding with the cleaning maid." He hoped Evans would move ahead, perhaps to speculating about the attempted bribery of constables that Timothy Gibbons had shared.

"The maid heard everything as well?"

"As much as I did."

"We can use her as a corroborating witness. Will she testify?"

"I believe so." He tried to shake off his discomposure. "She gave me her direction. I will interview her after noon. She planned to write down what she remembered."

"It's not every day that an ordinary London cleaning maid can write her witness statement."

"Phinney Darracott is far from ordinary, sir."

"Ah." Evans looked up from a file he had opened. "That's a name from your past. I suppose you will also discover her reason to be in London rather than your village of Brize Norton?"

The man's memory impressed Conrad. "She left Brize Norton several years ago, sir. Of late, she's had the care of her orphaned niece and nephew. I don't know the reason they're not at their home in Merrybush."

"Merrybush? Is that east of Nottingham?" He didn't wait for Conrad's agreement. "What's the family name? Not Darracott."

"Her sister married Peter DeChambeaux, an attorney whose primary work was in Liverpool. They were killed in a carriage accident there, two years ago."

Those pale moss eyes gleamed. "I remember. A suspicious carriage accident, where the carriage and horses weren't damaged. It was described to me as a freak accident. The two passengers' necks were broken. I found that very suspicious—both having the same injuries? The driver having only a broken arm? Then the Liverpool Constabulary blocked us from interrogating the coachman. He disappeared before we could persist with our inquiries. I've never trusted the Liverpool enforcement since that day. The new magistrate has replaced many of the constables, so the rot's not as obvious."

"A deliberate carriage accident?"

"Or murder made to look like a carriage accident. As I said, we never had a chance to interview the coachman. We came too late to examine the horses. They were supposedly put down. The carriage looked as if it had been tipped over, not that it wrecked or toppled into that ditch. Too many questions, too few answers. And asking more questions only made the former magistrate angrier and less inclined to help us."

"I agree that the circumstances do sound suspicious. But, sir, what reason did the London Constabulary give for investigating an accident that occurred in Liverpool?"

"Reason? An attorney leaves *Titterstone & Montjoy* and removes to Liverpool only to die accidentally less than two months later? That raised a few whiskers of interest at White Hall, especially since DeChambeaux is the son of an *émigré* who was more than familiar with Claude Thierry. But we could prove nothing more, even after months of work. The investigation into the accident in Liverpool closed before Nazenby received notification from a man he has stationed there." Evans glared at the dead man on the floor. Had Titterstone blocked the investigation? How? He was miles and miles away, in London. "Hoppock, find something to cover him. Not decent, leaving him lying like that."

"There's a curtain in the closet, sir."

"Use it. I don't believe anyone will protest when they discover the reason for its removal."

He had the work of mere seconds to yank the curtain from its hooks. When he returned, the chief constable had his back to the dead man. He had selected a file from the shelves and slowly turned the documents over.

When Conrad encountered her last evening, Phinney had stood beside those shelves. Had she been searching, not cleaning? Even as he himself searched while he failed miserably at his pretense as a clerk.

Although Merrybush was miles away, Phinney was in London. She worked in the building where Titterstone and Montjoy had their offices. Her work placed her, for the long night hours, in the very offices where her brother-in-law had once worked. She worked alone, when no one would see what she poked into. Her brother-in-law and her sister died mysteriously not long after they removed to Liverpool.

Titterstone and Montjoy were on the shady side of the law, representing both Richard Malbury and his uncle, the infamous Boss Malbury. The Honorable heir was named in the confession of an executed French spy. Before he fled for the continent, he numbered French spies among his friends, chief among them the suave operative Claude Thierry, who still awaited trial.

And Peter DeChambeaux's father was an associate of Claude Thierry.

In his investigations, Conrad had learned that coincidences rarely occurred. Thin strands of sticky spider webs linked people who seemed to have no connections to each other.

What did Phinney hope to find? A clerk's copy of a letter to Liverpool, hiring someone to kill Peter DeChambeaux? No, that was too fanciful.

He remembered the old skirt that she'd worn, faded, frayed at the hem, the ruffled cap that had hidden her hair. If he hadn't known her so well, if he'd only given her a cursory glance, he might not have recognized her. Would Titterstone have done so? Had he ever seen Peter DeChambeaux's sister-in-law?

Phinney would need anonymity to protect her. The last person she had expected was someone who knew her well. When Conrad had recognized her, she'd looked flabbergasted. She should have expected someone would eventually recognize her. Brize Norton might be far from the main roads, but Squire Costell enjoyed his trips to London and often invited the *ton* for visits over the summer.

Those London visitors, the celebrated of the *ton*, were the very people who had enthralled Phinney on that long-ago day, when he wanted to tell her he was leaving Brize Norton and she wanted only to talk of the Costells' upcoming fête.

As he draped the curtain over the dead attorney, Conrad didn't ask his superior the obvious question of *You had eyes on Titterstone & Montjoy two years ago?* More than once his own investigations took longer routes to arrest and prosecution. "When I interview Miss Darracott, sir, I will have more questions than I anticipated, not just about her statement but also how she came to be employed here and the connection between her late brother-in-law and this firm."

Evans shoved the file back onto the shelf. Several other files slid, as if they wanted to join their mates on the floor. He carelessly propped them back. "We need a man in here, going through these files and ledgers. I don't believe Titterstone would leave his office in this state."

"The mess is Richard Malbury. He wanted a file that Titterstone refused to hand over. He threw files on the floor before he shot him and added more after, when he searched but didn't find what he was looking for."

"What file?" his chief snapped.

"One that Titterstone recently had stolen from an office in Liverpool. According to Malbury, his uncle is very interested in that file. Only—."

"What?"

"Well, Boss Malbury might want to dig a few hooks into Liverpool, but I don't believe he would. So, did Richard Malbury lie, to keep Titterstone from knowing exactly who wanted the file and why?"

"Who do you think wanted the file—if not the boss?"

"I keep coming back to the French spies, sir. Titterstone working for Malbury, who worked with French Spies. Pierre DeChambeaux, a known associate of Thierry until his arrest. Peter DeChambeaux worked for Titterstone until he removes to Liverpool. Then he's killed in Liverpool. Malbury returns. A file is stolen from an office in Liverpool. A man with a French accent tries to bribe Timothy Gibbons to be elsewhere. And Malbury shoots Titterstone for refusing to turn over this mysterious file."

"Spiraling events. The file is stolen two years *after* DeChambeaux dies. His office would have been closed long ago, everything closed up and disposed of."

"Not the files. He had clients. Any active cases would have transferred to new attorneys. Any closed ones would gradually work back into the clients' hands, or at least the hands of their new attorneys. Maybe it took two years to track down the file. It might have mixed in with unrelated files. Or someone just stored it with others and didn't unbox it until they had to search through that box. For whatever reason, it may have taken those two years to discover the incriminating file still existed. Has any other Liverpool attorney died recently, especially under mysterious circumstances?"

A gleam in his eyes, Evans nodded. "No one's asked that question. We'll get onto it—after we inform Kennedy Montjoy of his partner's death. I want you with me for that, Hoppock. We'll send another constable and a rector I trust to inform Mrs. Titterstone. I doubt she knows much. Then I'll inform Sir Roger of Malbury's involvement in these events. He may have a man fully cognizant of the spy ring that he can assign to these files. Once we can pull out the relevant documents—and locate this mysterious file from Liverpool, we may have everything we need for the Crown prosecutor. While I'm with Nazenby, you can interview Miss Darracott."

"Very good, sir. But—Peter DeChambeaux, are you certain he was murdered? I ask, sir, because that answer will shape the questions that I put to Miss Darracott."

"We were closing in on DeChambeaux when he was killed."

"He was working with the spies?"

"Not working with them, *per se*. Certainly knowledgeable of their actions. We know a Pierre DeChambeaux did certain favors for the first spy ring, the one run by Robert LeBrun and the woman Celestine Sourantine. Peter is the anglicized version of Pierre. That must be him."

"Do we know the reason that DeChambeaux severed his ties with Titterstone and Montjoy and transferred his practice to Liverpool?"

"That information never came up." Evans clenched his fist and pounded on the door's frame. "I want this case solved, Hoppock! Two murders disguised as a carriage accident. Two more murders, Stephen Phillips by drowning and Titterstone tonight. We were close two years ago, and we're close again. Whoever this French spymaster is, he protects his identity by killing anyone who might reveal him. I want this man. I want his assassin. I know the first crimes occurred in Liverpool, but it began here, on my turf. The poison is spreading now."

"Mr. Montjoy's reaction to his partner's death will be interesting, sir."

"Yes." Evans' thinned lips twitched. "A good word: *interesting*. Dawn is coming. We need to head for his residence. Have you a key for this office?"

"I have my copy of the master key, sir, cut when I first came here."

"Good. We'll lock the door on our way out. Mr. Gregory can admit the undertaker and our men when they return. Did you check Titterstone for his key?"

"No, sir." The task repulsed him. He knelt and fumbled under the curtain to reach the dead man's pockets. He found nothing in the jacket's outside pockets. The waistcoat's watchpocket had only a shilling. Drawing back the curtain, he unbuttoned the lawyer's brown coat and tried not to look at the greying face. An inner pocket had a folded paper but no keys. He opened the paper and held it toward the light. *B. 2D. Kirkgardie Street.* "What do you make of this, sir?"

Evans had nothing to say except "Another line of inquiry."

Conrad draped the curtain over Titterstone's head. "No keys," he said as he rose. "As I remember, sir, he tossed his keys on the desk." Evans' head swiveled round then came back to him. "Exactly, sir."

"Dammit. I need constables on the street, not guarding this office, especially when bribes may turn their eyes away. Gibbons is returning with the undertaker?" At Conrad's nod, Evans heaved a sigh. "He'll have to stay then. I'll pen a note and give it to Mrs. Gregory to pass on to him. We've questions that I don't want delayed."

Conrad wanted to linger, but he followed his chief. He locked the inner office while Evans pinned his note to Timothy Gibbons. The daytime hours were not the worry. With night would come Malbury. What was in that file from Liverpool?

And who wanted it so desperately? Boss Malbury, to inspect its contents and glean names? To win an edge over the criminal master of Liverpool?

Or was it financial information? Letters of credits and bonds. Access to bank accounts. A raft of money that would lift Malbury into the wealthy yet closeted life he claimed to want?

Was it information that would finally condemn Claude Thierry?

Or did the file name the identity and location of the French spymaster?

Malbury would return, he knew it. With the right man on watch, they could set a trap, let Malbury believe the office was not watched. He would walk in and find the file. Then they could swoop in and take him. They would have both murderer and file.

In his years on the force, Conrad had learned to have a skeptical eye for coincidences. He'd also learned that nothing came as easy as anticipated.

Chapter 8

Vic reached for the door latch, but it swung open before his fingers grazed the iron.

The giant Orion loomed over them. Arms folded over his barrel chest, he scowled. His thick bottom lip pushed out.

"Th-thank you, Orion." Elise elbowed past Vic and stepped up to cross the mission's threshold. "We worried that Vic might have to pick the lock," she added boldly.

Vic winced.

"Better the lock picked than the latch left off the hasp," Orion rumbled. Vic chanced a quick look up and saw the African's scowl. But he gave a nod to Vic, and the boy's tension eased.

"Oh, we would never leave the door unlocked. `Tis not safe." She kept her arms crossed over her thin chest, hiding the files under her shirt.

He grunted an agreement. "Are you coming or going, young Master?"

He cringed inwardly, but he couldn't convince Orion to stop naming a street tough like him *young master*. "Coming," and he stepped through the doorway.

Orion pushed the door closed, but he didn't drop the latch into place.

"Has my aunt returned?"

At his "not yet", Elise tossed a grin at Vic. She had argued that her aunt Phinney would never know they had snuck out. He hoped she wouldn't crow too loudly when they were upstairs in their attic rooms. Then Orion added, "She will not be pleased that you two were abroad during the night."

"Will you be a tattle-tell-all?"

"Not I, but Miss Darracott is coming along the street."

"Dash it! That's unlucky."

"Has Mrs. Stowbridge returned?" Vic asked, hoping the older woman would distract Phinney. "We left right after she did. What was she doing all veiled like that?"

At the second question Orion's brow descended into a fierce scowl. "You do not question or mention that, young master. The business of Mrs. Stowbridge has naught to do with you."

Elise saved him. "Has Mrs. Stowbridge returned? For I know my aunt wanted to speak with her. Something to do with our rent."

At the outright lie, Vic dropped his gaze to the floor, not wanting to betray her. He appreciated her defense. Even though no reason had occurred, Elise found the tall African fearsome. Her reckless streak showed, though, with that lie and the open look on her winsome face.

"Mrs. Stowbridge does not charge rent of Miss Darracott."

"It was to—to defray," she pronounced the word she'd remembered with glee, "our costs, for it's not just the roof over our heads but also the food we eat. Especially Hank. I think he's making up for all those lean months in Liverpool."

"The mite can eat all he wants. The mistress said it."

"But it's so-o-o much."

Orion chuckled. "Not compared to the plates I empty. Go on with you, little miss." He unbent enough to use a speck of cant. "I will delay Miss Darracott enough that you can hide what you have tucked under your shirt."

"Orion!"

"Scurry out, mouse one and mouse two."

She did, running up the stairs with Vic on her heels.

They stopped at the first floor, for Orion had again opened the door. They leaned over the banister to listen.

"Good morning, Miss Darracott. Are—have you been hurt?" His voice changed to a growl, an intimidating sound that the children hadn't heard from the giant.

"Does it show? I had hoped—no matter."

"You have dirt on your clothes, Miss."

"I do?" A pause, and Vic imagined Phinney Darracott brushing at her clothes.

"Did someone hurt you?"

"Not me, Orion. One of the lawyers—." She lowered her voice.

They missed her explanation, but not Orion's reaction. "Shot dead?"

Vic and Elise exchanged a look. Had Phinney just related that someone—a lawyer—was shot dead? Vic had not missed the stress of scrabbling a living on the streets, but since they had hied away from Liverpool, his life had been dull at ditchwater. Tonight, twice, death brushed close by.

"Yes. Yes, it's—appalling, I know. A constable will come here at noon, to interview me. Constable Conrad Hoppock. Do you think Mrs. Stowbridge will allow me to use the morning room?"

"That is not for me to say, Miss. You must request that of the mistress."

"I will. Please inform me when she breakfasts."

"She is in her office now, Miss."

"She is? Would she mind if I interrupted her?"

"I think not."

Elise waited until they reached the attic landing before she elbowed Vic. "We owe Orion a favor now. He's a good man, isn't he? To think I was so afraid when first I saw him."

Vic envisioned those fists as big as hams. The giant could crush them without effort. "He's a big bruiser." But Orion didn't look for reasons to knock people about, and he hadn't offered to give Vic a buffet, not once. "We don't need to cross him."

"Oh, I don't intend to." Her eyes rolled to him. "He knows you can pick locks, Vic."

"Hank," he answered her unspoken question. "Talking while he stuffs scones into his mouth. You going to look through those files now?"

"Yes. Ammunition." She jerked up her shirt and produced them triumphantly. "When Aunt Phinney rings a peal over us, I want to have more than one good reason backing us. I suppose you are going to sleep?"

He couldn't help her read the files. He could scarce write his own name. But he didn't remind her. "Aye, that I am." He stretched upward. "I need me beauty sleep."

She laughed then clapped a hand over her mouth, too late to prevent the sound echoing down the stairs.

. ~ . ~ . ~ .

Widowed a decade ago, Olivia Stowbridge still wore black weeds. This morning she also wore an evening gown, the scooped neckline embroidered with blackwork and jet beads that glistened with her every breath. A lacy shawl as black as her gown lay draped over the straight back of a wooden chair. Jet beads mixed with diamond-like jewels glittered in the lacework.

When Phinney entered, the woman looked up from a letter. Once again, her beauty amazed Phinney. Her mother had gone to school with Olivia Stowbridge, but while she lay cold in the ground, victim of a weak heart, Olivia was widowed and still hale. No silver marred her blonde hair, styled in a simple chignon. Only a close look would spot the fine lines around her eyes. The deep ruby curtains behind her, still closed against the increasing dawn and drifting fog, created a background worthy of a portrait.

"Josephine, are you returned already?" She glanced at the mantel where a clock ticked away. "Is that the time?" She brushed a hand over her hair although not a tendril was mussed. "Do take a seat. Tell me—I must suppose something has occurred that sends you to me this early."

Phinney sank into the upholstered chair. The desk's wide expanse was between them. The older woman claimed that desk remained from her husband's days as a shipping officer for a major firm, a worthy position although it meant his wife received nothing on his sudden death. The massive desk would have dwarfed even Phinney, who counted herself taller than most women, but the petite Olivia Stowbridge never seemed small when she commanded the mission from behind it.

She folded the letter and tucked it into a drawer. "This is London. Evil prowls the street, *seeking whom he may devour*," she adapted. "Tell me what has occurred."

Even with Phinney trying to limit her words, the whole horrible event poured out.

"Heavens," the older woman said when she described hiding in the closet, then "Good God" at the lawyer's death. "Are you certain this man—this murderer did not know you were watching?"

"I am *not* certain, especially since I believe someone followed me home. I managed to lose him in the fog, but—." Clutching her arms didn't stop the fear that shivered over her.

"Orion!" the widow called. The door opened immediately, proof that the giant had stationed himself to eavesdrop.

"Miss Darracott, did you see the man who followed you?"

"No. A little. He wore a light grey suit, like the man in the office did. That's the reason I connected them."

"Anything else?"

"He wore a red brocade vest. The worst of it, Mrs. Stowbridge, is that I do know him."

"The dead man?"

"Yes, but also the—the murderer." There. She'd said it. And by using that word, Mr. Titterstone's death increased its horror. Not death. Murder. Murdered. Murdered while Phinney and Conrad watched. "I met—."

An uplifted finger stopped her. "Orion."

"I will see to it, Mistress."

She waited until the door shut. They heard no footsteps travel away from the door, for the giant walked on cat-feet. "I do not know what I would do without him," Mrs. Stowbridge mused. Her cornflower eyes fastened on Phinney. "Now. What were you saying? That you know this man, this murderer?"

"I met him." She marveled at the coincidence when her life had had so few. "Several years ago he came to Brize Norton, to a summer fête given by the Costells. He came from London with his friends. I met him several times. He must have stayed a month or longer."

"He would recognize you?"

"If he remembered me. He has no reason to remember me," she

added with simple honesty, neither proud nor humble. "I was not impressed with his talk of London society. Father had just fallen ill. My thoughts were on him." And on a certain young man who had soon left the village without telling her. A young man who would come here at noon. No longer so young, he was grown to a sturdy constable, broad of shoulders and quick of wit.

"Tell me his name," the older woman demanded.

"Richard Malbury."

She sank into her chair. "That is a name I have not heard for several years. I do know he fled England a couple of years ago and has lived abroad. Belgium, I think." She tapped a finger on the desk blotter. Then her pale eyes lifted and speared Phinney. "Who did he kill?"

"George Titterstone."

She gasped then fell to coughing.

When the spasm continued, Phinney leaped up and dashed to the sideboard. She splashed cordial into a glass and carried it to the desk. Mrs. Stowbridge took it, managed to control the cough enough to take a sip then another. She coughed again, cleared her throat, and drank more of the fortified wine, emptying the glass. She waved Phinney back to her chair.

"I am shocked. Obviously." She swallowed, trying to remove the scratch in her voice.

Phinney settled on the front of her chair. The widow's shock had dampened her own. She knew it would surface again. She would have nightmares about Titterstone's eyes. But a heavy and curious weight of calm had settled over her.

Not calm, she reasoned. *Determination. Here is Titterstone dead. Once a partner with Rosie's husband Peter. They were murdered. Why wouldn't Titterstone also be murdered?*

For the same reason? For something he knew? For that file? What did he know that Peter also knew?

The file taken from Liverpool. An old case file of Peter's?

She wished she knew. She wished to read the file.

Tonight. Tonight she would return to Titterstone's office. She would find that file and discover that lethal connection.

After Conrad interviewed her.

"Will Mr. Titterstone's death interfere with your plan?"

She looked up and realized Mrs. Stowbridge had said several things, and she heard only the last. "Will it? No," and she realized that was one truth among many. "His death makes me all the more determined to find the answers. I have to," she added ruefully, her mind tracking to the two imps scurrying up the mission's steps, "or Elise may tumble into trouble."

The widow's brow contracted minutely then cleared. "Ah. Orion told me that she had gone out last night, with only that boy Vic to accompany her. He wanted to know if he should track them."

"Did you tell him *yes*?"

"No. I would have stopped her had I known earlier. He informed me when I returned from my own errand."

Phinney glanced at the lacy shawl with its glittering brilliants, but she didn't ask.

This mission is filled with secrets, as many secrets as the whole of London holds.

"I doubt you could have stopped Elise," she opined. "I don't think she *is* stoppable when she is resolved on a course others would call imprudent. I brought the children with me to London because I knew she would find a way to get here on her own."

"Yes. She is very like her aunt."

Phinney's eyebrows shot up. "Me? Not at all."

The older woman gave a slight shake of her head, but she didn't argue. "What do you plan now? You were investigating Mr. Titterstone, weren't you? How can that continue now that he is dead?"

"You should replace *investigating* with *snooping*. I think that's more appropriate. The trail does not end with Mr. Titterstone. He has a partner, also an equal partner with my brother-in-law."

"Mr. Montjoy."

"Yes, Kennedy Montjoy. I see that you are familiar with the firm."

Mrs. Stowbridge opened the drawer where she had secreted the letter, stared at the contents, then shut the drawer. "And Richard Malbury? Will you report him to the authorities?"

"The Constabulary is already aware of Mr. Malbury's guilt. They also seek him for his involvement with French spies, here in London, if you can believe it."

Mrs. Stowbridge gasped and fell to coughing again. When Phinney rose to fetch more cordial, she managed to stop the spasm. "No, nothing more, please." Pressing a hand to her throat, she swallowed several times. "Do sit down, Phinney. I mislike you looming like that. Do you think your brother-in-law was involved with these French spies, just as Richard Malbury is?"

She subsided but kept her perch at the chair's front edge. "I cannot believe that he was. His father's involvement makes more sense."

"His father?"

"You never met him, did you? *Monsieur* DeChambeaux wasn't a devotee of the *ancien regime*, as most of the other *émigrés* from the French revolution were. His main hope, though, has always been to recover the family lands. He bent my ear every Christmastide with his schemes to petition Bonaparte. I do know that Peter had a falling out with his father only a few months before their deaths. I wonder if he holds the crucial piece to this puzzle."

She had never expressed all those thoughts together, but now that she had, they made an odd sense to her.

The widow's pale blue eyes seemed to watch her avidly. "Whatever you need, Josephine, you know that I will help you."

"Thank you, Mrs. Stowbridge. You are doing so much already. I cannot ask——."

"Nonsense."

The door opened, preventing anything more. Orion entered, a looming presence. "I searched the streets all ways, Miss Darracott. I saw no one matching that description. I did not see any strangers at all."

"Oh, wonderful! Thank you, Orion. I did hope that I had lost him." She stood. The clock chiming the hour gave her an excuse. "I have taken too much of your time. And I must tackle Elise about leaving the safety of the mission."

She must re-arrange all the puzzle pieces she had gathered and mix in Pierre DeChambeaux's pursuit of his family's lost lands. Had that pursuit led him to associate with French spies?

"Orion will walk you home from your work tonight," Mrs. Stowbridge offered.

"No, Liv, I stay with you." He stopped abruptly, but those few syllables opened a wealth of meaning.

"Just this once," she said calmly.

"Once is all it would take," he growled, cryptic words that would have spun Phinney's mind into a dozen ideas if it weren't swirling with the puzzle of Pierre DeChambeaux.

She brushed at her stinging palms. "A constable will come today, to take my statement about poor Mr. Titterstone's death."

"Should Orion tell him that you are too overset for this statement?"

"No. Oh, no. Conrad would never believe that. He knows me. He's from Brize Norton. He was a simple plow boy when I knew him. He came to London years ago, to become a Bow Street Runner." The words tumbled over themselves.

Mrs. Stowbridge gave a Madonna smile. "A plow boy who has become a constable. He does not sound so simple to me."

"He's not. I mean, he never was. I teased him—oh. Just call me when he comes. May I use the morning room for the interview?"

"Of course. Any of the public rooms are at your disposal."

"Thank you. You are so kind to us." She'd said too much. She would start babbling soon. "And now I have two children to convince that their efforts will only hamper mine."

.~.~.~.

Vic heard the light footsteps and expected Aunt Phinney to fling open his door. He imagined the names she would call him. The blame should land on his shoulders.

The door did open. The words weren't harsh, though. "Vic? I have tea and boiled eggs and scones in my room. Join me. Elise and Hank will be there, too."

He sat up. "Me?"

"Yes. You're not going to escape my wrath, you know, going out at night in London!" She sounded appalled, as if the capitol were worse than Liverpool's waterfront streets.

She didn't know the worst of Liverpool, though. Vic had ensured that neither she nor the children encountered it. It had grazed close but never touched them.

They had described their own encounters with evil, burglaries and arson, threats, the man who jerked up Hank by his shoulders and shook him hard. Nothing like what Vic knew.

He climbed off his pallet, though, jumped into his breeches and shoved bare feet into his good boots before following Phinney along the hall.

When he shut the room door and turned around, it was to see Hank blowing on his tea to cool it and Elise seriously drizzling honey on a buttered scone.

He joined them, sitting cross-legged on the rug before the hearth, a cheery little circle of warmth while the fog thickened like grey smoke outside the attic window. He looked up at Phinney Darracott and wondered if he would ever understand her. "I thought you were going to light into us."

She grimaced then shrugged. "I fully intended to roast both of you. I've had time to re-consider. Elise tells me that she's found evidence." She handed him a bowl with an egg and passed him the salt.

Hank sighed happily when Elise handed him the honey-covered scone.

"Tell me, Elise."

"Someone could be listening," she hissed.

"No. No one's in the hall," her aunt said firmly. "We agreed that I would search the office of Titterstone and Montjoy. I didn't agree that you would hare off on your own search."

Elise twisted her shirt, unchanged from the night's adventure. "I remembered something. I thought Vic and I could go without any trouble. And we did. No one laid a hand on us."

Vic focused on his egg rather than mention the watchmen who had tried to corner them and the fire that had helped them escape.

"I brought back several files." The girl's blue eyes shone. "And there's more boxes to go through. Papa's old files. Documents that weren't tossed out, the way they were in Liverpool. Boxes and boxes of files."

"Where?"

"A warehouse on Kirkgardie Street, near Bell Tower Quay."

"You never mentioned this place to me."

"I found it, in that file that I took from the office in Liverpool."

"What office in Liverpool?" Her voice had a scary darkness. "Elise Helena DeChambeaux, I want an answer."

"I—I—."

Vic intervened. "I worked a job in Liverpool, before we left. Picking locks to get into an office. I didn't know it then, but the man who hired us was that Mr. Titterstone."

"This is the job that led to the deaths of your friends."

He didn't call them friends, especially Joe, who had had a heavy fist, but "Yes. And the reason we left Liverpool."

"Only to run into Titterstone at that great house," Hank inserted.

Phinney's gaze shifted from Vic to Elise then back. "Your friends took something from a locked desk. And Elise," her eyes pierced her niece, "you also took something from that office. Which theft caused their deaths? The file Titterstone wanted? Or the file that Elise took?"

No one answered. Vic finally said, "No way to know, I guess."

"I guess," she repeated. "May I see this file, Elise? The one from the Liverpool office? And you might as well bring the ones that you took from the warehouse tonight. Have you collected any other evidence that I should know about?"

"No," they chorused.

"Get the files," she ordered, "and I've information to share with you. Something horrible that happened tonight. You had better hear it. Perhaps you will be more cautious."

Vic remembered Button's hand, fallen from the pallet, no longer covered by the shrouding blanket.

Murder. That's the horrible thing she meant.

Chapter 9

Elise plonked several files into Vic's hands. "I thought she was going to blast us."

"Something must've changed her mind. She may still," Vic warned. He recognized the Liverpool file in her hand. The rope that closed it was blue, not red like the others.

As he followed her back to Phinney's room, he stared at the files he cradled, filled with words he couldn't read. Lockpicking in Liverpool was boatloads easier than those squiggly letters. Once he got his reputation, the money had come in good but not steady. He reckoned letters and ciphers would earn steady, maybe not so good, but those jobs didn't risk gaol or transportation.

Or crossing the boss who controlled all criminal activity in London. After last night, Boss Malbury would know a new lockpick worked London. Breaking into the warehouse screeched lockpick and uncommon thief, one interested in documents rather than items for quick sale. Vic had opened a rusty lock and an inner door. He'd started a fire. Aye, he winced, the Boss knew all that, and he'd be looking for London's newest thief.

With the boss alerted, with the traps and snares of London to navigate, that left him the strait and narrow, as Phinney called it. Ever since he'd taken the three Darracotts under his wing, fledgling ducklings crossing the dangerous waters of petty crime, Phinney had preached a better life. Vic weren't no fool. He knew she directed those sermons at her niece and nephew. And her better life meant more than buttered scones drizzled with honey.

Were the scones worth the strait and narrow? Or had he fallen into a trap? Did knots of sentiment bind him, tighter than big anchor ropes on merchant ships?

He watched Elise open the blue-tied file for her aunt. Loosened from its pony tail, her hair fell like a waterfall over her shoulder as she slowly turned the pages filled with writing he had no hope of reading.

A sharp knife could cut those anchoring ropes of sentiment.

"Is this everything that was in the file?" Phinney asked.

"Yes. And in the same order. Look! This paper has Papa's name and signature. This one has several notes in his handwriting. See? This one, especially."

"How do you know this is your father's handwriting?"

Elise reached under her shirt. She fumbled then came out with a square note, a blue wax seal broken in two. The note unfolded easily, the paper softened with use, thinning at the creases. She held the paper beside the document.

Phinney drew in a quick breath as she saw the note's contents. "Yes, I see. This was his last letter to your mother?"

"I don't have any of her letters."

"Well. This is clearly his handwriting." She turned back to the file as Elise carefully folded the note and tucked it away. "I suppose you've read every word in this file several times."

"A dozen times and more! But there's nothing there."

"I wouldn't say that." She lifted a paper. "You surely saw this. *B. 2D. Jardin Parterre de le presbytère.*"

"I don't know what that means," Elise admitted. Her forlorn voice drizzled over Vic, making him wish he had the solution to all problems.

No, he wouldn't be cutting his ties to the Darracotts. He'd stay and keep them away from the sharply-toothed jaws of the underworld. Once they returned to their world of buttered scones, he'd find another road.

"We haven't kept up your French lessons. Your grandfather will be disappointed that you cannot chatter to him in French. What do you think *jardin* means?"

"*Jardin?* Garden? *Jardin parterre* would be a partitioned garden, with boxwood borders and flowers planted in different places. Mama planned to have a *parterre* at Merrybush, only she called it a knot garden."

"A true parterre is on a grand scale. A knot garden would have been very pretty. I wish … ." She didn't complete the wish, just looked back at the paper. "*Presbytère* is another word for church, especially a non-Catholic church. *Jardin parterre de le presbytère* is a church garden, and that is—."

"Kirkgardie! How did I not see that?"

"What is B and 2D?"

Elise's brow furrowed into funny wrinkles. Vic offered, "The warehouse was the second on from the church garden. The office we broke into was on the first floor, fourth along."

"An easy code," Phinney said, "once we understand what it's talking about. I still cannot believe you ventured to this warehouse alone. You should have told me. Both of you," and her sharp gaze focused like a kestrel on Vic. He squirmed.

Elise planted her hands on her hips. "You didn't listen when I said I knew where to look. You focused on those two lawyers, especially since they were at Parton March. Those murders had nothing to do with us."

"True. But there they were, lawyers who knew your father, working with unscrupulous people who committed murder. One of whom you had seen in Liverpool, your mustached man, Vic. Involved with more murders, for didn't you believe they ordered the deaths of your friends Joe and Button? Mr. Titterstone was the reason we had to leave Liverpool—and then we encounter him at Parton March where we hear of more murders. The man was the center of death." Her mouth twisted. Vic wondered what information she held back. Something that she didn't think Elise and Hank needed to hear. She turned over several papers in the file. "How did you remember the name of Kirkgardie Street, Elise?"

"Last week. Mrs. Stowbridge asked me to post those letters, remember? One of the addresses was Kirkgardie. Then I remembered Papa taking me there, only a couple of weeks before we left London. Once we found it—."

"We?"

"Vic and I."

Phinney's brown eyes narrowed. "I don't want you roaming the streets of London. You could be stolen."

"Vic knows—."

"Vic knows Liverpool. Not London. Or am I wrong?" and once again that kestrel-keen gaze fastened on Vic.

"You're not wrong," he admitted.

"No more dangerous than Liverpool," Elise argued, "or have you forgotten the press gang?"

"No, I haven't forgotten." She worried her bottom lip then said, "Mr. Titterstone is dead."

"He died?"

"He was shot. By—well, the name will mean nothing to you, but Richard Malbury shot him."

"Malbury?" Cold steel pierced Vic. "Like Boss Malbury?"

"Yes, his nephew. Who is Boss Malbury?"

He jumped up, turned toward the window, turned back. He looked at the door, at the cheery little fire, then finally back at Phinney. "The boss runs London. He runs the criminals."

Her color faded. "Worse than I thought," she said faintly. "I should have left you three at Parton March, as I tried to do."

Elise shot a look from her aunt to Vic and back. Then she touched her aunt's arm. "We would have followed, as we threatened to do. If you wouldn't let us stay with you, then we could have stayed at Grandpapa's, even if he is away on business."

"Why?" Hank piped. He'd remained silent throughout, first because of the scones then because he had nothing to add. Vic hadn't forgotten the boy, but Phinney started as if she had.

"What?"

"Why did he shoot him, Aunt Phinney?"

"Mr. Titterstone wouldn't give him something that he wanted. Something that his uncle wanted," she amended. "I don't know what."

"And this Richard Malbury shot him?" Elise asked, now as pale as her aunt. "He shot him dead? How do you know?"

"I saw him. I was hiding in a closet. He didn't see me. He didn't even know I was there." But her eyes shifted guiltily, and Vic reckoned she was hiding more information. "A constable will be coming soon, to interview me about what I saw."

"That's the reason you were back a little early?"

"Yes. I think I know where Mr. Titterstone keeps that file. I could have retrieved it, but not with the constable there and Mr. Titterstone lying there, staring—."

"Mr. Titterstone and the file in Liverpool. And now Mr. Titterstone is dead, killed by this Richard Malbury."

"Hsst," Vic warned. "Not so loud, Elise." The giant Orion ghosted along the halls. They only knew where he was when he let them get a look at him.

Her gaze darted to the door, then she nodded.

"Aren't we safe here?" Hank whispered. "Vic, aren't we safe?"

"I don't know," he said, and that was honest.

"Nobody can get past Orion," the boy said stoutly. "Nobody can get past Mhambi in the kitchen."

"Who does Orion really work for?" Vic whispered.

"Mrs. Stowbridge."

"And who else, Hank? She goes out at night," he confided to Phinney. "Orion goes with her. He didn't go last night, though."

"What are you saying?" she asked.

He shrugged. He truly didn't know, just that something was off, something he wanted a thumb on. He wouldn't be able to find it, let alone fasten it down.

A sharp thwack sounded below. They all jumped.

"A door blowing shut," Phinney explained.

Aye, Vic thought, that could have been a door blown shut. But there was no wind. The fog drifted slowly beyond the window, enclosing the world in its vaporous cloud. Someone had slammed a door. Someone who was angry and wanted other people to know.

Orion kept a rein on his temper. Wouldn't be him. Maybe the cook, but Mhambi rarely left her domain. The maid Liyana? Or Mrs. Stowbridge.

Or maybe one of the wounded veterans on the second and third floors. A sturdy wall on each floor separated the mission hospital from Mrs. Stowbridge's private residence. The wall divided the building, but sometimes the children heard screaming and groaning and arguments. At the mission the veterans had their physical wounds tended until they were well enough to return to the world. If they didn't heal, the doctors sent them to the manor in the countryside.

Maybe an orderly had slammed a door. Maybe he was angry at a doctor's order.

But Vic doubted anyone on the wards had slammed a door.

"Well," Phinney started only to be interrupted by her niece.

"I think the answer is in Papa's files," Elise whispered.

"They were destroyed, child."

"Not the ones in the warehouse on Kirkgardie Street. There are more than ten boxes. We need to go back. We can go back tonight, Vic, and—."

"No." He hated to disappoint her. When Elise whirled to face him, he explained, "They'll be watching. We can't go tonight. Not tomorrow night neither."

"We have to go back! They'll be looking for what we were looking for."

"They won't go into a locked storeroom," he argued. "They'll be looking for what we were looking for. They don't know we were upstairs. They came on us when we were on the ground floor, not before. We can wait a few nights."

"They'll look!" she countered. "They'll look everywhere, even if they have to hire a lockpick. The answer is there. It has to be. It's nowhere else."

"Wait." Phinney closed the file and rapped it on her knees to get their attention. "I think what Richard Malbury wanted is still in Mr. Titterstone's office. I don't think anyone will discover where he hid it. I will get that file tonight. How many boxes in the warehouse, Elise?"

"Eleven," she said definitely although Vic thought it was more.

"Then we'll need a wagon and men to haul out the boxes. Orion can help us there." She held up a hand to stop arguments. "He doesn't need to know where we're going or why. We'll go this afternoon."

But Orion shook his head when asked by Phinney, Vic and the children arrayed behind her, like ducklings swimming across a pond. "No, Miss Darracott, not today."

"That's disappointing. The children have—they have been without those things since their parents' deaths two years ago."

It weren't exactly a lie, Vic reckoned. It wouldn't count. Phinney hadn't crossed her fingers behind her to ward off evil for the almost-lie.

The giant's harsh features softened as he looked at Elise and Hank. "It's not possible this afternoon, Miss. I would have to hire the wagon and horses and a couple of men to help."

"I have coins that should cover the expense."

She touched her high-necked blouse and Vic remembered her pendant, a woman's profile in white on a pale blue surface. A cameo, she'd called it, when she saw him staring at it. A gift from her mother.

"Will you set everything in motion for tomorrow morning then? Early, please, Orion."

"Yes, Miss. How early?"

"As soon after sunrise as possible, I think."

His eyes widened, the whites showing all around, but he didn't complain. "Will that be all, Miss?"

"I need a good jeweler. Does Mrs. Stowbridge have one?"

"Brixton and Briggs, on Alford Street. That's off Bond Street, Miss."

"Goodness, I'm not certain I have clothes fashionable enough for that district. Perhaps Mrs. Stowbridge will lend me a pelisse for the afternoon?"

She herded the children back to the attic. As Elise and Hank trooped back to her room, Phinney caught Vic's arm. "I need you to spy out any strangers, Vic."

"What?"

"During my meeting at noon and after, when I must go to the jewelers, I want you to watch for any strangers around the mission. Don't approach them, Vic. Just watch them. We need to take better precautions."

Chapter 10

With sunrise, the fog first thinned then thickened, obscuring even more than before. Airless and dank, neither warm nor cold, the vapor hung on the streets, obscuring distant views and dampening passing sounds. Only years of tromping through London on a nightly beat helped Conrad maintain direction. His chief Evans had hesitated at several turns and accepted Conrad's guidance without question.

The weather prognosticators claimed the fog came from warm air over France, an unstoppable invasion across the colder Channel waters.

The fog's invasion struck Conrad as ironic, for Napoleon's promised invasion had never materialized. Now the deposed emperor wasted on the Mediterranean island of Elba. He hoped this summer also saw the defeat of the French spies, lingering in London as if they expected their emperor to retake his throne and resume his attempts to turn all of western Europe into his personal footstool. He said nothing to his chief. Evans' singular focus for the past season had been the arrest of the French spymaster.

Kennedy Montjoy resided in a newer terrace of houses near Hyde Park. Painted white, the brick façade seemed to absorb the fog. Black railings sweated the clinging damp. The brass door knocker and fittings glistened from the hours of vapor.

Evans mounted the three steps and pounded on the door. Hands behind his back, Conrad watched the street. No one passed. At this early hour, the workers and tradesmen kept to the main thoroughfares and the narrow byways leading to the gardens and servants' access behind the houses. They avoided the streets before the terrace houses, for the workings of the city were shielded behind their own fog from the elite citizenry that depended on their regular deliveries of staples and fuel.

Evans knocked again, louder and longer, then dropped back a step. "Your case, Hoppock. You take the lead. I'll interject when I see a need."

"Sir. Thank you, sir." The chief's approval shone radiant after the gloom of last night's murder. Conrad's chest swelled with pride. He was clearly advancing up the Constabulary.

While they waited for the door to open, Conrad tracked over his path to this doorstep. When they met with Montjoy, his disguise as a clerk would collapse. Evans had men appointed to trace Montjoy after they left. He expected the solicitor to panic. He hoped the man led them higher up the chain of French spies.

A handful of months ago, Conrad hadn't known spies operated in London. He worked theft cases, tracking leads to capture burglars who focused on high-value items owned by the wealthy. Pursuing one lead to a fence, he discovered a cache of rubies and small diamonds, broken up from a parure. In deeper trouble, the fence babbled the location of the burglar. After the arrest, Conrad followed his nose to discover the source of the jewels. The small jewels were not identifiable, but a large teardrop ruby in a gold setting surely would be. He carried the pendant to a posh jeweler on Bond Street. The man recognized the piece. After Conrad claimed that he wanted to return the set to its owner, the jeweler pointed him to the maker of the entire parure.

The second jeweler gave him the purchaser. That man, a minor lord who had blustered about until he realized Conrad was stubbornly waiting for answers. Then he called in his wife, a well-spoken woman with auburn hair. She claimed to have lost the entire set while playing cards, "and debts must be honored, Collinwood," she explained to her dumb-founded husband. Conrad wanted the name of the man she'd lost the set to. She didn't give up the man, but her husband helped, demanding to know the whole along with any jewels that she'd lost at the tables. Conrad left them shouting at each other and carried his investigation to the man—who tried to flee when Conrad identified himself. A few questions later, and he had the story of a series of payments with rubies and diamonds to several *émigrés* scattered throughout London's high society. Those names matched to names he'd seen on a list in Evans' office—for Conrad had the gift of reading upside-down.

When he carried his information to his chief, Evans dragooned him to ferret out more information. By watching, drifting along the streets or catching hacks to follow carriages, he slowly built the strands of a network. He couldn't find the spinner of the web, but he knew enough to knock the web down. At his next conference with Evans, in May, his chief explained the case. Although Boney had abdicated, French spies still worked in England, hoping to destabilize the government enough for the Corsican general's return. In a dark-paneled office of White Hall, he met the English spymaster Sir Roger Nazenby and his second, Lord Giles Hargreaves. June saw Conrad dragooned to arrest a known spy, only to have the man killed before he could be apprehended. August landed Conrad the clerking position with *Titterstone & Montjoy, Solicitors*. He'd tracked names like DeChambeaux and Poulaine, Audley and Stellensgard. He hadn't found a whiff of connection with the London crime boss, but he fully expected Henry Malbury to be the spinning spider.

Especially since his nephew Richard Malbury had worked with the

French spies and had used mysterious resources when he fled to the continent to escape arrest.

Now he stood on the bottom step, waiting to enter Kennedy Montjoy's residence and surprise the man into betraying a few snippets when he learned of his partner's murder by Richard Malbury.

Evans re-mounted the top step and reached to hammer again, but the bolt thunked back. He dropped his arm as the door opened a few inches. A sallow man with drooping eyes appeared. He wore servants' livery although his cravat under the high-buttoned jacket was undone. "Sir, the house is not yet receiving." He backed a half-step.

Evans caught the door before it moved an inch. "Chief Constable Hector Evans," he identified. "My second, Constable Hoppock. We must speak with Mr. Kennedy Montjoy, the solicitor. Immediately."

At Evans' rank, those baggy eyes opened wide. "Sir. I am not certain—. The master is not awakened before ten of the clock."

"He will be awakened much earlier today. Are you the butler?"

"The third footman, sir. Havers."

"Bring the butler. And admit us. I'm not standing on this step like a beggar."

"Sir, your pardon, sir." He fell back, and Evans and Conrad entered.

The fog invaded with them, clinging to their wool jackets and hats, adding dampness to the stuffy air of the hallway.

Without directing them to a receiving room, the footman shuffled off, heading for the back of the house. Conrad peeked around until he saw his chief openly examine the furnishings and appointments. Then he didn't try to hide his own assessment of the polished brass fittings, the many-branched candelabrum on a side table, and the oriental vase figured with red dragons, a stark accent against the saturated blue walls. The candleflames didn't flicker. Their light glinted on the gilt wall sconces and the frames that surrounded somber denizens of previous generations, solemnly watching the two men. A patterned runner protected the entry. Beyond its edge was a diamond-design parquet. Conrad did not know an exact figure, but he knew enough to reckon the hall's decorative appointments would pay his salary for a couple of years and more.

But he saw a cobweb attached to the corner of one painting and drifted dust along the floor molding. A lax mistress? A lazy housekeeper? Or signs of scrimping in the pay of servants?

Brisk footsteps heralded the butler's appearance. A stiff man with grey frosting his temples and his dark hair combed back and clubbed at his nape, the butler mimicked the denizens who watched from the walls. Although he wore the same livery as the footman, his tailed jacket was longer. White gloves protected his hands. A sneer protected his position.

"Chief Constable … Evans, is it?" He looked from Evans to Conrad then back. When Evans nodded, the butler turned, cutting Conrad out of the dialogue. "I am Connaught. Mr. Montjoy remains in his private chamber as yet. I will inform him of your visit."

"Not good enough, Connaught. Inform your master of our arrival. We come direct from the office he shares with George Titterstone. The matter is of great urgency."

Connaught's dark brows rose. "Has the office been burglared?"

"Has their firm experienced that difficulty?"

"I have no direct knowledge of that answer, Mr. Evans."

"Chief Constable will do, or Chief Evans. I would rather not stand about in this hall. Is there a receiving room? We will wait there while you inform Mr. Montjoy that we must see him."

The butler hesitated.

A sound in the back hall caught Conrad's attention. He saw the second footman, tie and jacket now properly done up, as well as a skirt peeking around the corner.

"Here, sir." Connaught opened a door on the left. "I will personally inform Mr. Montjoy."

"Do that," Evans agreed, not ceding any authority to the man.

"Should the matter concern Mr. Montjoy's law offices in partnership with Mr. Titterstone, Mr. Montjoy will wish to know that his partner is also informed of this urgent matter."

"Mr. Titterstone is well aware of it," Evans retorted although only Conrad understood his mordant dryness.

The butler dipped his head, not finding them worthy of a bow before he backed from the room. He left the door open, clear indication that they were not to be treated as welcome guests.

"Montjoy's done well for himself," Evans commented after a quick perusal, this room painted with the hall's deep blue. More gilt touched the pale-painted furniture upholstered in linen with stripes of blue and gold. Gold tassels decorated the curtains, similarly striped. More ancestors overlooked the visitors, these with ruffled collars like the kings and queens in the museum paintings.

Evans stepped lightly over the faded geometric carpet and checked the hall before returning to Conrad. "Remember," he whispered, "you take the lead."

"He'll know I've spent the past month clerking for his office," he reminded, his voice equally low. "I've taken orders direct from him."

"We'll deal with that when he comments on it. And if he doesn't comment, that will tell us quite a few things as well."

Light footsteps in the hall, unlike Connaught's brisk steps or the footman's shuffle. A maid appeared, carrying a tray laden with a ceramic teapot and cups. "Tea, sirs. Mr. Connaught's orders. To take away that foggy chill."

"Our thanks, to you and Mr. Connaught," Evans promptly said. He followed the young woman to the low table before a settee and two side chairs. "You'll play Mother?"

She giggled but poured their tea.

Evans took an upholstered chair with spindly legs that didn't look as if they would bear his slight frame. Conrad, taller and sturdier, eyed the matching chair and the plump silky fabric of the settee then chose to drink his tea standing up.

His chief asked a few questions of the young woman, "how many of the servants were disrupted by our early arrival" and "had the Montjoys returned late the previous evening".

"No, sir, they dined in. Mr. Montjoy had a client in his study—a lady dressed all in black, with a lacy veil over her face. She came at midnight and didn't leave for a cou—."

"Becky." Connaught's stern word stopped her light flow. "Back to the kitchen with you. Take a tray up to the mistress."

"Yes, sir," she squeaked. She dipped a curtsey before scurrying away.

The butler turned to them. "Mr. Montjoy begs a quarter-hour, Chief Constable. Please ring if you need any assistance." Then he retreated, shutting the door.

Evans calmly sipped his tea.

"A visitor at midnight," Conrad mused. "A lady all in black. A widow?"

"Coincidence or connected to our investigation, that's my question. What time did the encounter that you witnessed occur?"

"The small hours, sir. Well after three o'clock. I may have had my head stuck into a payment ledger, but I did hear the case clock on the second-floor landing."

"Did you know your friend was there?"

"I knew the maid was cleaning. I saw her from the back, mobcap and apron, with a basket and broom, but I was concentrating on this old ledger. Mr. Bannockburn, the chief clerk, usually keeps them all locked away. I've scoured through Fulbright's easily enough. The old man had the ones that I needed to scan intermingled with Clements, Pickard, and Quincy."

"Deliberate?"

"Possibly. Low-level, if anything." Conrad didn't want the low-hanging fruit. He wanted the top men, the traitors who didn't care what happened to their countrymen and the profiteers who committed theft and blackmail and murder, all while they passed information to the French. In scarce supply were the true French compatriots, the ones eager to revolutionize Britain as part of the Bonaparte empire. Only the Russian winter had managed to defeat Napoleon. The general's forced abdication had overset the spies' grand plan, yet they continued on, as if their general would escape and once again use his army to play nine pins with European countries.

Conrad despised the arrogant members of the British aristocracy. He watched with hope then despair when Parliament rejected much needed reforms. At all levels of life, good men and bad fought to control the government. Let Boss Malbury and French spies and shysters like Titterstone and Montjoy grasp the reins of power, and England would fall.

Although Titterstone would never climb into the golden phaeton to touch those reins.

Conrad wanted to stop the bosses and the traitors and the shysters. Then he'd go after the people who aided and abetted their crimes.

"Deliberate, for certain," he agreed with his chief, "and I'll ask those questions at the appropriate time. I would like to discover who this mysterious lady in black is, see where she leads us. Now, though, we have a murderer to catch."

The door opened as he spoke. Connaught looked shocked at Conrad's words. He composed his features. "Come with me," he droned.

Yet his gaze skittered sideways. *Looking for escape? Thinking to send a warning?* Conrad didn't know, but he would bet Stiff-stick Connaught would spread the word as soon as he escorted the unwanted visitors to his master.

Chapter 11

Kennedy Montjoy's nefarious dealings with the criminal underbelly of London had rewarded him, yet cracks in the foundation continued to appear as Conrad and his chief climbed behind the butler to the first-floor landing and on to the private second floor. Cracked plaster joined the cobwebs. Faded curtains and unpolished brass told of lingering pinched purses. The solicitor and his partner Titterstone had amassed wealth to afford a lavish home, but the gushing spate of golden guineas had dried up.

A decade ago Phinney warned Conrad that money didn't ensure happiness. Perched on a weathered fence rail, wild roses scenting the air, and green trees framing her wind-tousled hair, the skinny vicar's daughter had shaken a finger at him in his plowboy's faded shirt and drill britches. "Mark my words, Conrad Hoppock. Put all your efforts into money-grubbing, and you will regret it."

"Sounds like one of yer da's sermons," he retorted, using his broadest country accent.

A circlet of braided grass stems hit him in the chest. "It's the truth. Happiness doesn't come from having wealth. Look at the Costells," the owners of the large estate where he'd spent the past weeks plowing from dawn to dusk. "All the guineas you would want, and none of them are happy."

"Might be that their unhappiness ain't got nothing to do with their abundance of gold. Besides," he dropped the dialect that she claimed was unworthy of the village boy who could out-cipher her, "I wasn't thinking of them. You and me. My only prospects is plowman for other people. A tenant farm won't come open for years. And you, vicar's daughter, what are you going to do if no one offers for you?"

"I'll keep house for my father."

"And when he dies?"

"My sister will give me a place. I know she will. Or I'll be a governess."

That plan had fallen apart, for here she was in sooty London, working as a cleaner, dropped far below her former gentility.

She would have soon learned that money stopped all sorts of problems that interfered with the happiness of her and the two—no, three children.

Why did I remember that?

She might wear a mobcap and an apron that swallowed her, but all

hia old yearnings had flooded back along with the rush of protection
and a wish—.

Maybe she had married?

No. He was certain she hadn't.

But that third child?

The butler opened a door with panels of robin's egg blue and stiles
lightened with a lemony wash. "Sir. The two constables."

"Any messages?"

"No, sir, not yet."

"I wish to be apprised immediately."

"Yes, sir." Connaught stood aside as they entered. Then he shut the
door without a snick of the lock.

Sipping from a fragile teacup, Kennedy Montjoy stood by a
window that overlooked the street. A silken cap of the same burgundy
silk as his robe sat jauntily on his hair. Underneath the robe he wore a
linen nightshirt. He lifted one eyebrow as he surveyed Conrad's blocky
frame in fog-damp wool and sturdy boots that served well for tromping
London's night-dark streets.

"Well?" he snapped. "What is it? Connaught said you claimed the
matter was urgent. Something at the building where we have an
office?"

His chief clasped his hands behind his back, clearly letting Conrad
take charge of this interview. He caught back the servile bow that old
training had wanted to give. He covered it by removing a handsewn
notebook from one pocket and a pencil from another. "I am Constable
Hoppock, Mr. Montjoy. This is Chief Constable Hector Evans. We've
come direct from the office you share with George Titterstone."

"Hmph. *Share.* Titterstone is my partner. Are you treating him to
such an early morning visit? What has happened? Has old Malbury
kicked the traces and escaped his handlers? Or has he died?"

"Old Malbury?" The name linked up with Richard Malbury and
confused Conrad.

"Lord Malbury, man. One of our clients, for all that he's senile.
Has to be watched day and night so he won't wander. Is it old
Malbury? Is he dead? I will have to notify his son as soon as possible.
The son's abroad. Brussels. Well? Speak up, man."

"Richard Malbury is in England, Mr. Montjoy." He hated his
deferential tone. Antagonism would only rile this man, but Conrad
didn't like presenting himself as subservient to a man he had no respect
for.

The solicitor's eyes widened in surprise, his first true expression.
"How do you know that?"

"I had occasion to see him last night." There, that was the strategy
he needed. Informative, emotionless. "Are you aware that Mr. Richard

Malbury is charged with treasonous acts?"

"Charged, not convicted. And on the evidence of an executed spy who was in all probability telling every lie possible in order to save his own skin. Didn't help him, poor bastard."

"You have sympathy for an executed spy who was connected with several murders and admitted to attempted murder?"

"I have sympathy for any man executed. I understand LeBrun kicked for a half-hour. Horrible way to die." He pressed a neatly folded handkerchief to his lips. "Mr. Richard Malbury is our client, but I also represent His Majesty's government. If I see Mr. Malbury, I will report that event to the local constable."

"I have no doubt that you will, sir, as a representative of His Majesty's government."

"Is this the reason you dragged me from my sleep at dawn? To inform me that a client has returned from his trip abroad."

Evans rocked forward. "Hardly a trip abroad. Malbury fled before we could arrest him. Did you warn him that a warrant was issued for his arrest?"

"How would I have known that? I have no connections in White Hall. I know no one in the Home Office."

"Yet you know the warrant was issued from the Home Office rather than a magistrate's court."

Montjoy's mouth opened and closed, a landed carp gasping for air. Then his eyes narrowed. He gave a single nod. "It would be the Home Office, wouldn't it? Young Mr. Malbury was accused of collusion with French spies as well as attempted treason. I haven't looked at the case in several years. My partner Titterstone handles these cases. Have you arrested Mr. Malbury? Mr. Titterstone needs to be informed."

"Mr. Richard Malbury is not in our custody."

"Then what necessitates this early morning visit? You did not come on business about either of the Malburys——."

"I didn't say that, sir."

"You said that you came direct from our offices and that the matter is urgent. I can only surmise that something has happened at the office. Have we had a fire in the clerks' department? Has old Malbury given up the ghost?"

Conrad would have sworn the man's eyes gleamed with that last question. "No, sir, not a fire, and nothing to do with Lord Malbury. And Mr. Titterstone will not receive a visit from us. I must inform you of a shocking event. Would you care to sit, sir?"

"I will not. Tell it to me. You've wasted enough of my time."

He hadn't prepared gentle words to break the news. "He is dead, sir. Your partner, Mr. Titterstone."

"Dead?" Montjoy's eyes didn't blink. "Dead ... how? A carriage accident?”

“No, sir. He was murdered. Shot in his office.”

“Good God. Shot? No. Dead? That’s not possible.”

“I witnessed it, sir.”

“You witnessed? How were you there? Wait, I recognize you. Hopson. One of the newer clerks. But you said you’re a constable.”

He was quick—or Titterstone’s death hadn’t shocked him. Either he knew of it or had expected it. *Or wanted it.* “Yes, sir, I was employed with you briefly as Connor Hopson, but my name is Conrad Hoppock.”

“Why is a constable clerking for us?” He directed his offense at the chief constable.

“He followed my orders,” Evans said calmly.

“*Your* orders? What gives you the right to position a constable in a private firm? We conduct no actions for the local constabulary.”

“My orders come from the Home Office. I directed Hoppock’s duties to fulfill those orders.”

“The Home Office? You’re back to young Malbury and French spies again? Really, gentlemen, even *if* Richard Malbury has returned—.”

“I saw him. I heard Titterstone identify him.”

“Even so,” Montjoy scarcely paused, “the young man has scarcely had time to re-connect with any alleged French spy ring. The men he knew—one is dead, the other remains in prison. How can he connect with that ring?” He argued as if he stood before judge and jury. “And he certainly did not kill Titterstone. He depended upon Titterstone.”

“Nevertheless, sir. Richard Malbury fired the pistol. He threatened Mr. Titterstone repeatedly. He wanted him to hand over something. Then he killed him. The bullet entered Mr. Titterstone’s skull.”

“No.”

“I witnessed it, sir.”

“No, you are mistaken. The person masqueraded as young Malbury—.”

“As I said, Mr. Titterstone himself identified him as Richard Malbury.”

“And you witnessed this? He shot his solicitor in front of you?”

“They were not aware of my presence.”

“Hiding, were you? Where? In that closet? Good God,” he repeated. After a long moment, he asked, “His wife?”

“One of my officers is informing her as we speak. I understand that your wife and she—.”

“They are great friends.” Forgetting his earlier statement, he sank into a chair. He leaned his head back and stared at the ceiling. “Good God,” he said again, as if he could think of nothing else. His eyes closed briefly. His hands gripped the arms of the chair. He shuddered once. Then his eyes opened, back to that antagonistic calm. "What do you want of me? I can set forward the funeral arrangements for his wife. How else can I help you?"

Evans unclasped his hands. "When Richard Malbury contacts you—."

"He will not."

"When he does, send word to us, Mr. Montjoy. He will count your life as cheaply as George Titterstone's."

Montjoy shook his head. He heaved himself up and crossed to the hearth to tug on the tapestry bell rope hanging beside the mantel. "Titterstone's death will leave a gaping hole in our affairs. I must acquaint myself with his specific cases, especially the case going to trial next week. What more do you want?"

Hidden from Montjoy's view, Evans' hand leveled, and Conrad held back his additional questions.

"What more?" his chief asked. "I would know the name of the lady who visited you at midnight."

"No," he snapped. "She came at great risk. Her case has nothing to do with you."

"We can be discreet."

"You'll clomp about in those thick boots and endanger her. No. She has nothing to do with Titterstone or Richard Malbury."

"Assure me that she has nothing to do with French spies and Henry Malbury, and I won't pursue any further."

"I—am unable to do that."

"Her name?"

"No. Not today. Not here."

Evans gave a curt nod. "Your word?"

"For the little worth that a constable would have in it—yes, my word. And yours, that no more of your constables will lurk about my offices or my residence."

"Hoppock will no longer pretend to be in your employ." Evans turned on his heel. "We're leaving, Hoppock."

"Yes, sir." He scrambled to open the door for his chief.

Questions crowded, most of them about the mysterious lady.

Then he saw the aquiline features of a footman ostensibly dusting the tops of painting frames. Their questions about the mysterious lady did not need to be heard by anyone except Kennedy Montjoy.

Chapter 12

Hank hared off to the kitchens as soon as his aunt permitted. "I'm late for my lesson," he explained.

"It has to be here," Elise muttered. "It has to be."

Vic wished it was—whatever it would be. Yet he kept seeing the other boxes, the ones too heavy for him to move. If he had to hide something, he'd stuff it into the last box but one, near the bottom of a heavy stack.

"Or it is with Mr. Titterstone," her aunt countered. "Perhaps Mr. Titterstone pulled the strings of—well, everything."

"Like a puppetmaster?" Vic remembered market days in Liverpool, with puppets on sticks, like Punch and Judy with their abuse and humor. "Directing from behind the booth?"

"Yes, like marionette dolls, controlled by strings. Mr. Titterstone. Mr. Montjoy. Maybe they had something on Peter, and he fell in with their plans rather than stand against them."

"Papa would not let himself be used to hurt others!"

"He would," Vic defended this man he'd never known, dead these two years. "The man you've talked about would have. To protect someone else."

Phinney lowered the document and rubbed her eyes. "I didn't consider that. Rosie never explained Peter's abrupt move to Liverpool, but if he were protecting someone—."

She dropped the paper to the floor then crossed to her bed and knelt. Vic thought she would search between the thin mattresses, but she reached under the bedstead. She groped about before uttering a satisfied sound. When she stood, she clutched a paper folded into a square. The paper didn't crackle as she opened it. Time and use had softened it.

She scanned the close writing as she returned to her chair. "Yes. Rosie writes that Peter was concerned for his father. She doesn't give a reason."

"Concerned for Grandpapa Pierre?"

Dark eyes lifted to meet the pale ones of her niece. "Pierre DeChambeaux. And his son Peter, who anglicized his name."

"Pierre is Peter in English, ain't it?" Vic's stomach went hollow. "You think somebody confused the names? The old man got crosswise with someone, and the son paid the price?"

"Dear Lord, I hope not. They could have killed *M'sieur*

DeChambeaux, and we never learned of it. If this is what happened, then I am very glad your grandfather did not take you and Hank into his care, Elise."

The girl's brow creased. "He wasn't in London. He was on business in the Duchy of Warsaw. That's what the solicitor who came to the house said."

"The Duchy of Warsaw?"

Vic didn't know where that was. He hoped the country hated Boney as much as the Brits did.

"He wrote us when he returned." Elise's voice quavered with the memory. "We were already with you then, at the Benwicks, when his letter arrived."

"I do remember. He said he would come if you needed him, but he must leave again on business in a fortnight. In my reply I explained that the house in Merrybush had burned."

"I wrote him. He didn't respond," the girl said flatly.

"But his neighbor did, remember? His letter returned with yours enclosed. He said your grandfather left unexpectedly."

Vic sorted out the pieces. "So, when he came looking, if he did, you weren't where he could find you. This Merrybush place had burned, and you didn't stay with these Benwick people. You came on to Liverpool."

"Yes, for their house was burgled, just like the Squire's."

"And Merrybush," Elise added, her voice small and trembling, "before they burned it down."

Phinney refolded the letter. "Maybe we should visit your grandfather, Elise. I am certain his direction would not have changed. We could look him up tomorrow."

"If he's in London. If he's still alive."

"First I must meet with Constable Hoppock. And I must change. Tomorrow we retrieve the boxes from that warehouse. Then we'll look for your grandfather." She rose, thrusting the folded letter into her pocket. "Heavens, after months with no clear direction, we've a lot to investigate."

Elise sprang up and clutched her aunt's hand. "Should you meet this constable alone, Aunt Phinney? I mean—is he safe?" she added with a whisper.

"Conrad Hoppock? Of course he is. We grew up together in Brize Norton. I trust him. Off with you two, for I must freshen up and change."

Vic helped Elise gather up the files. They trooped across the hall to her room, leaving the door open so the narrow room didn't become stuffy. She spilled the files to the floor and knelt beside them. "I'm going to read through these again, especially the parts that mention

Papa. And look at his notes. Maybe his comments will make more sense when I read them thinking about Grandpapa and not Papa."

"I'll stick with you."

"You'll be bored."

"Got nothing else to do."

Her smile slipped away too quickly. "What if the answers are in the other files? Those men at the warehouse *know* we were there."

"They don't know where we were. They don't know what we took."

"They saw us at the stairs."

"At the stairs. Not up them."

"They'll have all day to search. And all night."

"Not them," he scoffed. "They'll be accounting for what burned. And shifting around what didn't burn to make sure no sparks remain. They won't turn to looking for where we might have been until much later today. They won't find it. I didn't scratch the lock or the plate. They never saw which office we were in."

"You think so?"

He gave a solemn nod and crossed his fingers behind his back.

.~.~.~.

Phinney patted a cloth to her face and neck. The cold water revived her briefly, but she would need a pot of tea to keep going.

As will Conrad. He had likely not managed any sleep.

A tap on the door startled her. "Aunt Phinney," Elise called, "Orion says that constable has arrived."

"He's early!" yet as she cried the words, the bells of the church three streets away began to toll the noon hour. "Elise, ask Cook to have strong tea brought to the morning room."

"Yes, Aunt."

Her thumbs confused her fingers as she laced and tied ribbons. She had no reason to be flustered. A few brief smiles, a flashing look quickly diverted away, and nothing repeated after Mr. Titterstone arrived with Richard Malbury. Conrad seemed glad to renew their acquaintance. *Don't read something into a welcoming smile*, she scolded herself.

Six years ago, he was just as darkly handsome, with straight shoulders stretching his shirts, taller than the other village youths, a determined jut to his chin and a wishful look to his eyes. Everyone called him *Plowboy*, including herself. Hers was a tease, though. The boys he bested in reading and ciphering at the grammar school intended the word as an insult.

She had known he borrowed books from Squire Avesbury. Conrad had never shared what he was reading. Phinney hadn't dared give him too much encouragement. Her father would have rung a peal over her head. Conrad Hoppock the plowboy had had no prospects. He would inherit nothing from the uncle who had taken him in. Although he had talked of joining the Bow Street Runners, that seemed a fanciful dream. Yet she had cheered on his plans. He was one of the few in Brize Norton who took an actual interest in the bony daughter of the vicar. Most avoided her, too afraid of the vicar who breathed fire and thunder in his sermons and thumped misbehaving children on their heads during the week.

That Midsummer, in the days before he left, she had tingled with excitement when Conrad joined her daily walks up to the Costell manor where she helped the squire's wife organize the upcoming fête. Her heart thrilled when he dared take her hand. Her hopes soared when he asked to spend more time with her.

But Mrs. Costell wanted Phinney to help entertain the newly arrived London visitors, come at her son James' invitation. When Phinney's father fell ill, just days before the festival, she had no time for lingering walks.

When her father recovered, days and days later, a temporary improvement, Conrad was gone.

And she had no time for such dawdling reminiscences now.

She had no mirror to check her appearance. Her one pretty dress with cream lace over aqua silk was years out of fashion and fit her only because she had lost so much weight while in Liverpool. Her wavy hair fought a smooth chignon, so she jabbed in pins to force it to stay.

The cook's haunting song in her native African filled the stairwell and hall as Phinney reached the ground floor. She pinched her cheeks for color. Liyana tottered along the hall with a tea tray twice too large. The Delft china in blue and white, with cups and saucers for two, chattered on the tray. The heavy silver tea service emerged only for Mrs. Stowbridge's important guests. Phinney darted to open the door to the morning room, receiving a nod of thanks from the maid.

She grabbed three deep breaths before following Liyana. Her foolish heart still thumped loudly. Hopefully, serving tea would bridge any awkwardness with Conrad.

He stood at the window, in a navy jacket and trousers, the same that he'd worn last evening. Bright sunshine had evaporated the fog, and the early afternoon light streaming from behind him created a glare that obscured her view of anything more than his height and those broad shoulders.

Liyana set the tray on the low table before the settee. She poured a cup and handed it to Phinney who offered it to Conrad. "Tea? Strong and hot. Do you take cream or sugar now?"

"No. Black as ever. Thank you." He accepted the cup, and she turned to take the second one, which the maid had creamed for her.

"Liyana, I believe we will need a second pot in a half-hour. Unless," she appealed to Conrad, "that you think this interview will conclude by then?"

He gave a quizzical look, one mobile brow lifted. "No, we won't finish our conversation in a half-hour. The tea is welcome. It will brace me. I haven't slept. Have you?"

Phinney shook her head, directing her attention to the maid. "A second pot then, Liyana, in a half-hour, please."

"Very good, Miss." She curtsied and bore away the silver tray.

The bridge of tea was crossed, and Phinney had no idea what to say next. To start baldly with Mr. Titterstone's death seemed a solecism.

After a sip, Conrad set the cup back on the saucer with minimal sound. "This is an interesting household."

"It's a mission, administered by Mrs. Stowbridge. She gave us rooms."

"A mission for freed slaves?"

"No. I mean, Liyana and Orion—the man who would have admitted you—and Mhambi the cook, they *were* slaves, but Mrs. Stowbridge freed them when her husband died."

"They remain with her as servants?"

"I think—better the *known*? But that's a guess. I do not know."

"How are you acquainted with Mrs. Stowbridge?"

"She and my mother were great friends. The year after Mama died, Father allowed me to stay with Mrs. Stowbridge for a few months. I don't think he wanted me to disrupt Rosie's household." Hearing her chattering words, she clamped her mouth shut.

"Please accept my belated condolences for your parents' deaths. And your sister and her husband."

"Oh. You needn't—I mean, the grief is no longer so overwhelming." What did one say that wasn't awkward? Phinney realized they were still standing. Feeling a gauche girl just out of the schoolroom, she waved vaguely to a chair. "Please, sit. I never intended to keep you standing."

Conrad waited until she sank onto the settee before he took the chair to her right. He had no flourish of coat-tails that a dandy would have employed. "How long have you been here at the mission?"

"Less than a fortnight."

"The children came with you?"

"I could not leave them with strangers," and she thought guiltily how she had tried to do that until her conscience pierced her to the core. "I am their only relative. Well, except for their grandfather. We have not managed to discover if he is in London. He is often away on business."

"Have you worked at the offices as a cleaning maid since you arrived in London?"

Her excitement deflated, sagging like a balloon that lost air. Conrad wasn't asking these questions as a friend. The official interview had begun. He had launched into it as if he had no time for any pleasantries, and no wish to inquire into the intervening years.

Conrad had no desire to re-acquaint himself with foolish Phinney Darracott.

"No, not since my arrival. My employment started only a few days ago. Mrs. Stowbridge helped me to the position." Phinney remembered how the older woman had not even blinked when she hatched her plan to break into the offices of Titterstone & Montjoy. She had merely asked for a few particulars. "Mrs. Stowbridge is acquainted with the custodian Mr. Gregory. He was a patient here, like so many wounded soldiers who return from their service in the Peninsula. On her recommendation, Mr. Gregory hired me as a cleaning maid."

"He named you *Mrs. Coates.*"

"Oh. Yes. That was a bit of subterfuge. I did not think he would hire a single lady. He thinks I am a war widow with children, and working as a cleaning maid would bring in the coins necessary to support the family."

Phinney omitted that her search for employment was solely targeted at *Titterstone & Montjoy.* She let Conrad assume that she needed the work, any work, just as she had let Mr. Gregory assume that. A single bit of deceit in a good cause. Her disguise as a cleaning maid would work for Conrad as well as it had for Mr. Gregory.

Conrad had emptied his cup. She set hers aside then lifted the Delft teapot, offering more. "Please." He waited until she topped her own cooling cup and set down the pot before he asked the first crucial question about the last night. "How do you know Richard Malbury?"

"Can we ever say that we *know* anyone?"

"Don't parse words, Phinney Darracott. You know me. I swear that I know you."

She scoffed. "Childhood playmates is all."

"More than that."

"How much more can it be? You left before I reached sixteen years."

"It's good that I did. The temptation was already straining the reins. Your father would have caned me out of his parish if I'd stolen the kiss I wanted."

At his declaration, her heart fluttered anew. "I remember a kiss you stole."

"I said if I'd stolen the kiss I *wanted.*"

Her cheeks flamed hotter. Had she misread him?

Yet while she fumbled on newly shaky ground, he retreated to his brusque questions. "I ask again, how do you know Richard Malbury?"

"He is a passing acquaintance only. Do you remember your last summer in Brize Norton?"

"I have forgotten nothing of my time there."

Why do those words weigh so heavily? She could not decide if he had a personal interest in her. One moment it seemed so, the next moment she felt mistaken. Phinney scolded her tripping heart. "For the festival, you remember, the squire's son James invited several of his London friends."

"I remember you were all agog with the arrival of high society, too enthralled to listen to me."

The spice of bitterness caught her attention, but without opportunity to study it, she cast it aside. "Richard Malbury was one of James Costell's friends. He may still be, for all I know."

"I doubt it. I understand that most people cast him off when his name was linked with French spies. He had a few weeks after that information came out, but when his name entered in a warrant for arrest, he fled to the Continent."

"You've become better informed since last night."

"I've had hours to gather that information. My chief shared the file in his office. We have several particulars of interest. Did you spend time with him, Phinney?"

She laughed. "A high society buck spending time with a country vicar's daughter? I should say not."

"Will he know you?"

"That I do not know. Actually, Conrad, I spent very little time at the squire's after the London party arrived. My father fell ill."

He shifted position, then leaned forward to pick up the cooled tea. "I didn't realize his illness came so hard upon my leaving."

Phinney didn't know how to respond. She sipped her tea then continued to hold the cup to her lips.

He shifted again, crossing his long legs and resting the teacup on the chair arm. "Do you think Malbury will recognize you, or not?" When she merely shrugged, he pressed for more. "What do you plan to do next?"

"I beg your pardon? Next?"

"You should not return to those offices, not until our investigation is concluded."

"When will that be? When you arrest Mr. Malbury?"

"No. He is tangential to our primary investigation. I would not want you to return there, at all. It's not safe. I understand you walked home in the dark. That certainly isn't safe, Phinney. You should have hired a hackney coach."

"I cannot afford a hired coach every night, not with the few coins that I earn as a cleaner. Besides, not many coaches are about at dawn when my work ends."

"That's not safe," he insisted.

Phinney waited to hear more about his concern for her, but he retreated to his tea, using it as a barrier much as she did.

She wished he worried about her. Obviously, he was worried not about *her* but about his witness to George Titterstone's murder.

"Will you remain here at the mission?"

Once again, his turn of questions surprised her. "I do not know."

"This mission—. I assume people constantly come and go."

"Not so constantly. A couple of doctors have rounds daily. The orderlies on each floor come and go with their shifts. I do not believe many of the patients have visitors. Mrs. Gregory came to visit her husband while he had a bed here. She's spoken of it to me. Yet they are London residents. The families of most of the patients are far from London."

"And the patients themselves? Do you have much interaction with them?"

"Very little. The mission is separate from the house, you know. I did volunteer on the non-ambulatory floor when I first arrived. Once I took my position as cleaner, I had little time for that. Mrs. Stowbridge does have benevolent volunteers who come. They mostly read enriching materials to the patients or discuss plans and opportunities when they become ambulatory. Is that what you mean by *interaction*?"

"If Richard Malbury learned of your location—?"

"I doubt that will happen. As I said, I have very little contact with the patients or the employees or even the volunteers. Since he did not manage to follow me last night—."

Conrad shot to his feet. She gaped at him. "He *saw* you? He followed you back here?"

"No. I am not certain that man was him. Or that he followed me. I lost him in the fog, long before I came anywhere near the mission. I am not wholly without sense, to lead him straight to my home."

"You shouldn't stay here. It's not safe."

Phinney carefully set her tea down and clasped her hands, outwardly calm while opposing emotions played tug-of-war with her heart. "The mission is safe. Orion guards the door, and those who go to the hospital wards use the other entrance. The pass-door between the hospital and these private rooms is kept locked. *It's not safe*," she scoffed. "Where would I go? On my meager salary? And you want me to throw over my job as if I'd found a pirate's treasure chest. But I have not. I have the children as well. We are known here and quite safe. I will not move them among total strangers again."

"No, Phinney, this isn't——. Something will have to be done."

"Well, until I can manage a change of our circumstances, we will do very well here. Do sit, Conrad. You're giving my neck a pang."

Chapter 13

Conrad opened his fists and stretched out his fingers. Phinney wouldn't listen to his warnings, and he couldn't force her to do so.

For the first time, he looked at her present circumstances, not her past.

She lived here in the mission, obviously on the benevolence of Mrs. Stowbridge. He needed to inquire into that woman's background. Phinney also had care of her sister's children along with a mysterious third child. Her gown looked out-of-date, even to his fashion-backward eyes. Her clothes last night had had frayed cuffs, neatly sewn patches, and a threadbare hem. As a cleaner, she wouldn't wear her best, but her blouse and skirt looked long past good wear.

As vicar's daughter in Brize Norton, she had lived in the church manse, a comfortable living, for the Rev. Darracott was well respected in the Anglican church. On his death, though, the living would have passed to another minister. Conrad had thought widows and children received a stipend. Did they not?

"Where did you go, when your father died?"

Surprised, she blinked several times before she answered. "I became a governess."

"You didn't go to your sister in Merrybush?"

"No." That single word was void of any explanation. He wondered, but he didn't pursue the answer, not when she crossed her wrists and looked away from him, scanning the room as if she'd never seen it before.

Conrad knew that her brother-in-law Peter DeChambeaux had had a thriving law practice. Even though his death was sudden, he would have made provision for his widow and two children. "When DeChambeaux and your sister died, why didn't you keep the children at their house in Merrybush? Was he in debt?"

"Peter? He was shrewd with every shilling."

"Then how do you come to be here?"

"I explained——."

"No. I mean, why are you here rather than at Merrybush? I know DeChambeaux moved his practice to Liverpool, but didn't he maintain his country home?"

"Conrad, about my brother-in-law moving his practice to Liverpool——."

The door swung open. Liyana came in, bearing a second teapot on the silver tray along with plates of curious flatbreads stuffed with meat. Without a word, the maid bore away the cooling teapot.

When the door shut, Phinney sighed. "Obviously, Mhambi thinks we should not miss lunch. Have you eaten, Conrad?"

"I broke my fast after we informed Kennedy Montjoy of his partner's death."

Her brown eyes widened. "Not easy information to impart."

He resumed his chair then held out his teacup for refilling. He had to set the cup aside to accept a plate laden with the flatbreads. Phinney had taken only two. He intended to press two more on her, but by the time she poured her own tea and picked up her first sandwich—he had no idea what else to call it—he had scarfed down three, like the starving boy he'd been when he arrived at his uncle's farm. The meat had a savory hot spice, like a curry but hotter. A creamy spread balanced the meat's strange heat. He picked up the next flatbread. The opening offered peeks of the meat and spread. The aroma made his mouth water, and his stomach clamored for more.

He looked across at Phinney, delicately nibbling on the flatbread. He wanted to talk about this strange food, but duty demanded he discover anything that might impact the murder case. She would be the primary witness. Chief Constable Evans would not want any surprises ferreted out by Richard Malbury's barrister. "Tell me the reason you left Merrybush."

She winced. "It is a long tale," she warned.

"I'm in no rush, Phinney."

"It started with burglary and continued to arson."

"What?" He caught his plate before it tilted over and spilled the stuffed flatbreads. "Say that again."

"Burglary and arson. Merrybush is no more."

"Back up a few steps, Phinney."

"You know that Rosie and Peter died in a carriage accident in Liverpool?"

He didn't share his chief's comments on those deaths. He wondered if Phinney knew they were murdered. *Did that explain the reason she was in London?* "Go on."

"The children's grandfather was out of England at the time, so the solicitor contacted me. When I arrived, the servants were scaring them with talk of ghosts in the house."

"Burglars," he breathed, the flatbread forgotten. "How long before they gave up searching and resorted to arson?"

"You're quick."

While he wanted to bask in the praise, he couldn't tell her about his investigation. He merely repeated, "How long?"

"Less than 10 days after I arrived. Three weeks since Rosie and

Peter ... ." She trailed off. Her fingers tore at the flatbread, destroying the sandwich.

"The local constable—."

"Blamed an overturned candle in Peter's study. Or the kitchen chimney caught fire. He couldn't decide the source. But it's a curious fire that trails so quickly up the center of the front stair. We ran down the back stairs and found the housekeeper and two maids pounding on the back door. Locked from the outside. We had to crawl out the scullery window. Six people could have died, Conrad!"

"Where did you go?"

"A friend's house, in the village square."

He wanted to query *what friend*, but she glared at the memory, and he didn't want that woolly wrath directed at him. "How long before the next burglary?"

"The house burned on Monday. The first burglary at our friends occurred on Thursday with another while we were at church. And the next morning the cook found the coals from the kitchen fire scattered across the floor. Only by the grace of God had they not caught. We packed up and returned to Brize Norton, to Squire Avesbury."

"A good choice." He wondered why the squire had never mentioned that Phinney had taken refuge at his home. "Was there another burglary and another attempted arson?"

"Not for several weeks. The squire advanced us funds to replace our clothing. We settled in. I wrote to Peter's trustee, giving him our new direction with the request that he supply funds to reimburse the squire."

He knew what was coming. He shoved the plate onto the table, wishing he could have shoved all troubles away from her and two orphaned children. "How long?"

"A fortnight."

"Burglary? What then?"

"Squire Avesbury protested, but we packed up and left on the next coach. We went to my school friend Elizabeth Pickering."

"I remember her. Good Yorkshire girl. Red hair and freckles."

"Yes. Her Mr. Linton apparently finds them intriguing. Don't ask how I learned that bit of information. They have three children under the age of five. Imagine the nappies." She looked appalled. "Poor Mr. Linton didn't know what to make of Hank; he'd gone silent. I have Vic to thank for breaking him out of that behavior. Elise chased after Lizzie's two oldest. It was a lovely spring. I offered lessons in Latin and Greek to the boys at a local preparatory school. And I tried not to think ... ."

"About their deaths. For they had to be murders."

"Yes. Yes!"

"Why else the burglaries? Why else the arson? And why would they think you still had whatever incriminating evidence they were trying to find?"

"Yes! You understand. So many have not. But I wonder most about who *they* are."

"You're here now and not at the Linton's. What happened?"

"Mr. Linton returned from a trip to London to find his desk disarranged, his ledgers out of order, his lockbox broken open even though nothing was taken. He blamed Hank first, then Elise."

"And then you."

Her sharp chin dipped down. She sighed. "He believed me, eventually, but he said we put his family at risk. He was correct. I know that. Once the burglaries started, the attempts at arson would follow— and one might be successful, as it was at Merrybush. I didn't know how they tracked us—."

"Unless you wrote to the trustee."

"Yes. But I hadn't. Mr. Linton had." She sounded perturbed, her anger not so direction-less. "I did warn him—but he thought I was a silly woman with foolish ideas. I do take partial blame. I told Lizzie everything but not her husband. I only told him the broad sweep of events." She set aside her plate, one flatbread untouched while the other she'd demolished rather than eaten. The lid rattled on the teapot when she picked it up. She poured the tea quickly and set it down more quickly. Wiping her fingers on a napkin, she stared at the steaming amber liquid.

He wanted to fill that hollow look in her eyes. Loneliness had burdened her, given responsibility for two children while she grieved the deaths of the only remaining adults in her family. To realize they were murdered—she would want justice for them—but discovering the reason for their murders must have thwarted her. Without knowing the reason, she would never find the murderer.

Conrad wanted to commiserate with her, but dwelling on the grief wouldn't help her. Telling the rest of her story to understanding ears might. "How does Vic come into this?"

She brightened, even though no smile came to her wide mouth. "We met Vic in Liverpool. He's a gem—."

"Why Liverpool?"

"Elise. Don't look so appalled, Conrad. My sweet niece has the same analytical sangfroid as her father, God bless her. Peter had removed his law practice to Liverpool when he parted ways with Titterstone and Montjoy. Yes, that's an interesting connection, isn't it?"

"Were they his trustees?"

"The man who communicates with me is named Bannockburn."

He straightened. "Clive Bannockburn?"

"Yes. You know him?"

Conrad didn't tell her that man was the chief clerk to DeChambeaux's former partners. That was for later. "You were telling me the reason you went to Liverpool, that your niece prompted the move."

"She convinced me—and she can be very convincing—that the trustee might have closed Peter's office, but his case files had to be somewhere. The cases would have transferred to new solicitors, and his files would transfer as well. If we found those files, we might find evidence that would point the way to his killers. We arrived quite broke, though, and if not for Vic, we would have starved by the end of our first month. Vic kept us from falling into dire trouble."

"So, Vic is your third child," not her baby but an adopted waif, although her next words countered his image of a cherubic face, pale beneath smudges of soot and grime.

"Hardly a child. He is old in the criminal ways. I think he saved us more than a handful of times in our sixteen months there."

"Saved you?"

But she hurried on, and Conrad mutely swore to ask her later, much later, when those days in Liverpool were fogged by time. "Without Vic we would not have the only clue that brought us back to London. And here we are. I warned you that mine was a long tale. And my tea's gone cold. Your fault, Conrad Hoppock, for requiring me to explain our journey to this point."

"I accept full blame." Not once had Phinney mentioned a man who could have stolen her heart. Had anyone ever intrigued her? Set her heart to pounding just by his presence? She certainly increased his heart rate. He reached across the table, picked up her teacup, and dashed the contents into the waste bowl. Then he poured more tea, not steaming but certainly not tepid. He placed the cup carefully on her saucer.

"My hero," she murmured, her lips fighting a smile, her minx eyes watching his reaction.

He grinned, and she no longer fought her smile.

And his heart beat faster.

After pulling the bell rope, he returned to his chair, sitting on the front edge of it, leaning an elbow on the arm, giving up any pretense that he was a society buck at his ease. "Here's what I think—and what you must believe. Your brother-in-law was targeted. The snare for him tragically also caught his wife, your sister. Whoever murdered them expected his problems would end—."

"Only to realize that Peter had evidence that would convict this person when it reached the right hands. So they searched—or hired people to search."

"You don't think they searched for the evidence themselves?"

"If they had personally searched, they would know very quickly that Peter kept nothing important at Merrybush. He kept his work separate from his home life. He may have scattered his files from Liverpool to Kirkgardie Street, but he never took them home. No, I believe this person is a puppet master. They hired the murderer. They hired the burglars. When the searches were futile, they resorted to arson."

"Arson that would catch you and the children in the fire."

She shuddered and rubbed her arms, bare beneath the puffed lace sleeves of her once fashionable gown. "True. We escaped. And they continue searching. As I am," she added, so softly that he barely heard the words.

"And this puppet master is in London? Do you think Richard Malbury is connected to him?"

"You're back to French spies, aren't you? Because Peter's father and grandfather escaped the Reign of Terror. For years, *M'sieur* DeChambeaux has talked of nothing else but the restoration of the family lands. I know that Peter wanted nothing to do with his father's dreams. 'An old man's futile fancy,' that's what he called it. Your French spies are too convenient an excuse, Conrad. I think Richard's uncle is to blame. I think Peter had a document that could destroy Richard Malbury's uncle. That's the reason he was with Titterstone, to retrieve that document. And he shot Titterstone when he didn't turn it over. Titterstone and Montjoy represent more than Richard Malbury and his father, you know. They also represent the uncle."

"Henry Malbury."

"Is that his name? I only heard Boss Malbury."

The door opened. Liyana appeared, returning with the first teapot. "Mhambi says you'll be wanting more tea." She stared at Phinney's untouched cup and sandwiches, then she saw the waste bowl, filled with the contents of her second cup. "Miss Josephine, you're not taking your lunch." Retrieving the second pot, she poured the cooled tea into the pot and added the waste bowl contents. Then she set that pot aside, poured new tea into the cup, adding sugar and cream, which she handed across, holding it out until Phinney took it from her. "Maybe some sweet biscuits, Miss?"

"No. I have no appetite, but thank you, Liyana."

"Going hungry is not good for you, Miss."

"I know. I will eat later. Thank you for the tea. I do need that." She cradled the cup and saucer in her hand. "I most definitely need this tea."

"Drink up, do. But too much will keep you awake, Miss, although since you work the night through, that may be a good thing."

"Thank you, Liyana. That will be all."

"Yes, Miss. Sir."

Phinney waited until the door shut. Then her brown eyes closed briefly only to snap open and focus on Conrad. "Why are you pretending to be a clerk? Do you suspect that Titterstone and Montjoy are involved with French spies?"

"Softer," he warned. A nearby church bell began tolling times, counting the length of their meeting. He had more to ask her. If he was to report to the chief then set a watch on the law firm, he must soon leave.

"I found a note in Mr. Titterstone's desk. It listed an estate called Ridings in Little Houghton and a man names Charles Audley." Sipping her tea, she missed his reflexive jerk. "I have heard of a Sir Charles Audley, a classics scholar decoding the Egyptian hieroglyphs using the Rosetta Stone in the museum."

"A client," he lied.

"I don't think so, Conrad. On that note were also three words in a different hand. The name *Poulaine* and *cipher* and *key*. A man who can decode ancient texts would certainly find a modern secret message fairly simple to decode. He might even create an intricate cipher that one would need a key to understand. Maybe we should worry about French spies. Is Audley working for our government? Did the French attempt to kidnap him?"

Good Lord, with a few clues, she put together the scheme that had resulted in the death of the French master spy who had tried to kidnap Audley.

What was Titterstone doing with Didier Poulaine's name?

"Phinney, you can't go around talking of this with anyone."

"I haven't. Only you."

"Where is this note now?"

"Still in Mr. Titterstone's desk. You are after spies, aren't you?"

"Minx. Tell no one, you hear me? Please. I don't know all of the ends in this tangle. Spies. Murderers. Criminal overlords. I begin to think they're all entangled. And Peter DeChambeaux is the strand that will unravel the whole snarl."

She froze, her gaze glazed, then she blinked and sipped her steaming tea, and Conrad could almost imagine he hadn't seen that momentary stillness that betrayed a mental key unlocking the puzzling secret that had brought her to London.

He should press her for that key, but she looked exhausted. Although she had looked bright and fresh when she greeted him, she had wilted in the last half-hour, the half-hour that talked plainly of her sister's murder. He remembered how Phinney had idolized the older Rosie and how lost she seemed when Rosie married her handsome lawyer and left Brize Norton.

"I want to move you and the children. I will need to make arrangements."

"No one can find us here."

"Bear with me, Phinney. I want you safe. Did you not admit to me that someone followed you this morning?"

"I could have been mistaken. The fog——."

"Let's ensure your safety, yours and the children's. Unfortunately, this afternoon is too far advanced. I should have a location ready by tomorrow afternoon. Can you and the children be packed by then?"

"If we were going, we could be packed in an instant. Our possessions are so few, now. But we're not leaving the mission. I told you. We are safe here. You've seen how they look after us Anyone entering must pass Orion. His size alone intimidates most people. Liyana is constantly about. And Olivia Stowbridge would never let anything happen to us. We stay here."

He didn't argue. He would appoint a constable to watch the mission. Timothy Gibbons was trustworthy. Tomorrow, he would move them out of here, even if he had to move them into his own terrace.

Warmth unfurled at the thought of Phinney in his home, sipping tea and countering his points with her own—or joined together, as they had been this afternoon, building answers together, like partners.

She vowed she was safe here. He would trust that for one more night.

Chapter 14

Phinney watched Conrad descend to the street and walk away from the mission. He didn't look back. His mind had obviously moved beyond her and busily considered how to inform his chief constable of the new information he'd learned from her.

Burglaries and arson proved that someone was looking for an incriminating document. Peter and Rosie were murdered for it. The trail led from London to Liverpool, on to Merrybush and back to London—with poor Mr. Titterstone caught in the search for the document.

As she shut the door and ensured the latch caught, she realized that she hadn't shared her suspicion that Peter might have been murdered because he was protecting his father Pierre. She remembered starting to tell Conrad. Something had distracted her. She couldn't remember what.

Before he left, Conrad said an investigative auditor needed to examine Peter's files. Without mentioning the files scattered across her bedroom floor, Phinney promised they would be available tomorrow afternoon. He nodded, expressed his satisfaction with the afternoon, and took his leave.

But am I satisfied with that interview? She remembered too many missed opportunities. She wanted a present and a future, not a constant harking to the past. Conrad only wanted a witness to George Titterstone's murder.

Phinney placed her hand on the bannister to begin the climb to the third-floor attic. A door opened along the hall. She leaned over the railing and saw Olivia Stowbridge emerge from her office. Hand resting on her stomach, the woman appeared to be in deep thought, broken when she saw Phinney.

"Has your constable left?"

"He's not my constable, but yes, he's left. Just now."

"I did consider speaking with him," she replied, words that kept Phinney planted on the third step. "I have missed my opportunity."

The world abounded with missed opportunities. "Vic—," but Conrad would have reached the corner and headed off in one of three directions, and the boy had no clue to his appearance. She descended a step. "I wish you had mentioned that you wanted to speak with him this morning."

"I could not decide. I still have not." She fidgeted with the braided tassel off her yellow waist sash, the only touch of her attire that broke mourning. She wore a dark grey plain gown, not the full mourning of her regular habit, and Phinney wondered at the change. "Come into my office, Josephine. I think—I have information to give you. I believe you will find it pertinent. I know you came to London to find the killer of your sister and her husband. Come. I would not have us interrupted."

Phinney had shared only bits and pieces of her reason, but Olivia was an intelligent woman who could easily piece a pattern together. Curiosity piqued, she followed, catching up to the woman before she entered the room.

Sitting by the side window, his frame stretched out and his elbows planted on the cushioned arm of a side chair, was Orion. When Phinney entered, he sprang up. His eyebrows descended. "Mistress?" he asked when Olivia shut the door and turned the key.

"I do not wish our conversation to be interrupted."

"Should I wait outside, Mistress?"

"No, Orion, please remain. You know this sorry tale already, and I—I will need your strength."

"I could wait in the hall, watch for eavesdroppers."

"And who would do so in this house? Mhambi and Liyana are loyal to me."

"There's those about who have no loyalty," he pointed out. "The doctors might be caught up in their rounds, but the orderlies stray, as well we know," a statement that only increased Phinney's curiosity.

Who would spy on a benevolent widow whose only occupation was running a mission from her great house?

The question opened up odd paths of mystery.

Olivia motioned to the straight-backed chair before her desk. She remained standing, her fingertips splayed on the blotter. "What did your mother tell you about me?"

"That you grew up in the same village. Her father was the vicar, and your father served as a steward. She said you married well and came to London. And you were widowed … . When I came to visit, the winter after my mother died, I wanted to ask you what you remembered of her, but you had one crisis after another to resolve."

"That was a difficult year."

"Rosie had your address in her receipt book. Did she visit you as well, when she came to London?"

"We met occasionally, at dinners, once at the theatre, a couple of other times. I wanted to foster that relationship, not just because she was Serena's daughter but because her husband was Peter DeChambeaux. His star was rising with Mr. Titterstone and Mr. Montjoy, my own solicitors." She grimaced then sank into her chair. "I regret that I was unable to increase my friendship with Rosalind. She was very sweet to this turbaned woman who invited her constantly to teas and parties and drives in the park."

"I thought you knew her only through our mother."

Olivia's face had lost its usual brightness. She looked weary, haggard. "I played on that connection, once I realized it, but that came after."

"Then my head is stuffed with wool, for I do not understand what you're telling me."

"I shall be clear. And to do so, I must unveil things I prefer to keep in the shadows."

Orion abruptly stood. "I have work to do, Mistress."

"Sit, Orion. Bring your chair here, beside mine." He hesitated. Softly, she added, "So that I need only lift my eyes to see you, to draw on your strength. Please, Orion."

"Miss Josephine need not hear all this. She is an innocent, Livvy."

"And I would like to keep her that way."

He lifted the chair and planted it beside the desk, turned so he faced the older woman. "Say it then. Don't play Round the Bramble Bush and keep her in the thorns."

"I will. You stare, Josephine? Do you frown on my ... shall we call it friendship with Orion?"

Color heated her cheeks. "You are obviously friends. That I have always known."

"Orion has been my friend since the first weeks of my marriage. He is my bride gift, along with Liyana and Mhambi, given by my husband." Her voice hardened at the last word. "I have surprised you?"

"I thought your husband was in shipping, not the slave trade."

"He was. British goods to the Mediterranean. African slaves to the Colonies thirsty for cheap labor. Colonial goods like tobacco and rice here to England. No doubt, Mr. Stowbridge would still be shipping slaves if he had not fallen afoul of footpads. I thought I was freed—."

"Bramble bush," Orion muttered.

"Hush. She must know this part to understand the rest."

"Not all that shipping stuff."

"I did not intend to dwell on shipping. I have reached the debts my husband left hanging over me. A mortgage on this house," she cast her gaze back to Phinney. "But even with that mortgage, even with Mr. Montjoy demanding that I liquidate as many assets as possible, I freed Orion and the women. Mr. Montjoy was most displeased."

Orion pursed his lips at the smile Olivia gave him, and it melted from her weary face. "Brambly thorns."

Phinney broke the awkwardness with "I didn't realize Mr. Montjoy was your solicitor."

"Solicitor and trustee of my husband's estate, along with Mr. Titterstone. That's how I came to know Peter DeChambeaux and

Rosalind. I so wish that I had met her many years earlier. I wish I had met both of you before Serena died. I did not wish to introduce myself to Rosalind as Serena's friend. I hoped to add that into a later conversation with her, once she accepted the heavily-indebted widow Stowbridge into a closer acquaintance." She gave a wry smile at the deprecating description of herself. "That was not to happen. Rosalind began to have her babies and stayed more often at her home. Peter introduced me to his father, who charms everyone with that elegance from the *ancien regime*. And through Pierre DeChambeaux, I met Claude Thierry and Robert LeBrun."

Phinney's ears pricked up at those last two names. Where had she heard them? Was Olivia finally leaving the thorny brambles to get to the heart of her information? "Were you at the party Rosie gave, before she and Peter left London for Liverpool?"

"Yes. Still playing my part. Still trying to winkle an invitation to Merrybush from your sister."

A sinister bell tolled at those two bits of information, yet Phinney didn't know the reason it rang so ominously.

"But Rosalind's farewell party is several years ahead of my story." Her gaze dropped to her hands, hidden by the desk. In the silence before she continued, distant footsteps mounted the stairs, a woman sang a doleful tune, and a heavy wagon trundled over the street's paving stones. "Forgive me, Phinney. Orion has."

Whatever for? she thought, even as she watched the silent giant stretch a hand over the desk to the older woman.

"Always," he rumbled.

Her expression lightened. He truly was her strength, a grounding lodestone. She rested her hand on his, her fingers curled around his, mistress and servant and much, much more.

How had Orion become Olivia's friend in the first week of her marriage? Then she remembered the woman's hard tone when she spoke of her late husband, a man who obviously was not mourned, and she could guess at the treatment that had a young bride seeking help and a young man too compassionate to refuse it.

"I did say that my husband left debts, many debts," Olivia continued. "Selling this house would have paid them all, but we would be destitute. I was counseled——."

"By whom? Your solicitor?"

"By both of them. They wanted me to find an option that did not entail selling the property. This was in `01, Phinney. I had not yet reached forty. Some claimed I was still beautiful." Orion stirred. "Hush, you, it is a brief bramble this time. My late husband tied up the property somehow. I am still not exactly certain how, but if I married again, I lost this house. If I removed to another residence, I would lose it. I had to remain his widow, living in his house, to receive any benefit from his estate. Once that was explained to me, Mr. Montjoy had no trouble convincing me that the property was not a solution to my debts. He proposed—a different solution." Orion shifted and tried to draw his hand back, but she clung to it, to him.

Phinney winced and once again tried to bridge the awkwardness. "I imagine a widow who could not re-marry would have few options available to her. May I guess that someone introduced you to a protector?"

"I have not completely shocked you."

"I may be a vicar's daughter, but I am well acquainted with the few options available when a gently raised lady needs to earn coin. We have few positions open to us. I chose governess. You chose—."

"Lightskirt," she supplied. "I will not name the man who came to be my protector. Forgive me this one secret."

"But—how did you move about in society? You took me to a few quiet gatherings. I heard you speak of attending parties and soirées, even Almack's. How is this possible if you were … questionable?"

"This man did not move in the best of society. He was also not interested in parading me to soirées and the opera. Several weeks passed before I realized that his associates—." She stopped, swallowed visibly. Her grip on Orion's beefy hand tightened. "They were evil," she whispered. "He was evil."

"He hurt you?"

"No. He—others. He would laugh about it. He enjoyed revolting me with the information. He threatened—people dear to me."

"Boss Malbury?"

Olivia's eyes opened wide. "No! I know *of* him. I have *met* him. Mr. Malbury is *nothing*—. This man—I won't tell you his name," she repeated.

"Tell me how this man is connected with the deaths of Rosie and Peter?"

"The whole strand is tangled, but here's a strand you can tug on. The man who introduced me to Jacques was Pierre DeChambeaux."

Phinney seized on the name. "Pierre! That's Peter's father."

"Liv—."

"Yes. I know." She squeezed Orion's hand. "He worries about me. I was warned, you understand—or perhaps you do not."

"Warned?"

"Not long after I began my association with—well, I have given you his first name, have I not? Not long after Jacques became my protector, he warned me not to listen whenever he talked business, not to remember any conversations or anyone who visited him. If we met someone in at a public venue, like Covent Garden or a gambling den—

he liked the gambling dens—then those meetings were acceptable to remember. Any meetings at his home, though, those I was not to remember. And Pierre DeChambeaux introduced us at Covent Garden. So I can safely speak of that connection." Olivia directed the last statement to Orion.

"I do not like this. Miss Josephine need not hear all of this. She need not know your speculations. He warned you. You know he will inflict … consequences."

Her palm rubbed over his fingers. "I *have* severed my connection to him. We have talked of this."

"Argued. You will not listen. He never lets anyone free, not once he has a leash on them."

"I will admit that truth. But, Orion, I must tell her what I know."

Orion shook his head but did not protest.

And Phinney watched, fascinated by this glimpse of their hidden relationship. Did Mhambi and Liyana know? They would have to know. No wonder the household functioned more like friends than mistress with servants or employer with employees.

"I have often wondered how Pierre knew Jacques," Olivia speculated. Orion grunted and tried to remove his hand. She clung tighter.

"Tell her about yesterday. She does not need to know all of the past. Tell her."

She winced. "I am no longer under his protection, but occasionally—. It is as Orion said. He has a leash on me, and he uses it. Not often. Enough. And last night, he … tugged on that leash. He discovered—somehow he discovered—that I recommended you for employment with Mr. Gregory. Yesterday, he asked—."

"Demanded."

She nodded. "He demanded that I dine with him. A young man was there."

"Richard Malbury," Phinney inserted.

"How did you know? No, do not tell me. But you see, don't you? He wanted to know your whole story. I could not see—you should have told me that you suspected Rosie and Peter were murdered. When you wanted to work as a night cleaner for *Titterstone & Montjoy*, I thought you were merely tracking the children's inheritance. I never—."

Phinney stood. "What did you tell him?"

"Very little. He knew who you were. He said—he said, *Her little disguise does not work with me.* I think Mr. Titterstone must have seen you one evening, and he knew you from somewhere else—."

Even as her mind cast back, she asked, "Mr. Titterstone was there?" Then she remembered. Her second night as cleaning maid. The solicitor had entered the office as she dusted the shelves in the outer office. How had he recognized her when he had seen only her profile? "At Parton March. He saw the children and me, on the landing overlooking the entry, the night that we learned of the murder of one of the family who was still in London."

"Frederick Connolly, a grandson of Bennett Parton. You and the children were at his house in Shropshire?"

"We were sheltering there. With friends."

"You should return to them."

"We cannot. We will not."

"Sit, Phinney. I am your friend, not theirs." Orion shifted. Olivia glanced at him. Her gaze flickered to the door. "Perhaps you should stand at the door now," and she removed her hands.

He grunted and levered himself up, looking huge as Phinney sank into her chair. Giant that he was, he crossed whisper-silent to the door and opened it. Phinney saw no one in the hall. He didn't enter the hall, just shut the door and leaned against it. When she turned back to the older woman, frustration had furrowed her smooth brow.

"What else? What did you not want him to hear?"

"I have told Orion everything."

She tilted her head, not accepting that, but he said, "She has. Much though I did not like it. Liv, give her the truth."

"Very well. Jacques wants me to obstruct your purpose here. They want me to discover what you know, what you want. I told him that you were only interested in the children's inheritance. At the time, I believed that, so it was not a lie. And they accepted that I believed it. I hope."

"But you no longer believe it."

"I have heard too much. I have connected too many links."

"You cannot stop me, Mrs. Stowbridge. I will discover the reason that Rosie and Peter were murdered."

"I do not intend to stop you. I want to help you, but I am not certain what I could possibly do to assist you. And I will warn you. The more evidence you seek, the more danger you and the children are in. I would not want to see those innocent children hurt or ... worse because you will not stop. These men will protect themselves, Josephine. They care nothing about innocent children. I would never willingly endanger you and the children. Perhaps it would be better if they returned to your friends in Shropshire."

"They stay with me."

"I can understand your reluctance——."

Phinney thought of Elise's determination, but she didn't share that with Mrs. Stowbridge. "I know these men are evil, for they killed one of their own, didn't they? Richard Malbury killed George Titterstone. On the order of this man Jacques?"

"I do not know that."

"I would say so," Orion inserted. Arms folded across his barrel chest, he leaned against the door. No one could open it with his weight against it. "You and the little ones, Miss, you are in danger. Believe that."

"Did he order the murders of Rosie and Peter? He must have. As he must have sent the burglars to search the house at Merrybush. Then burned it down. He is still looking for evidence. Whatever evidence Peter has on him, it must be very dangerous. When Mr. Titterstone found that document in Liverpool—."

"What document in Liverpool?"

Phinney continued as if she hadn't heard the older woman. "He thought Mr. Titterstone would use it against him, as Peter must have threatened to do. So he had Mr. Malbury kill Mr. Titterstone. That was the order. Get the document and kill Titterstone. Kill Titterstone even if he doesn't hand over the document." She focused on Olivia. "The document is still in Mr. Titterstone's office. Should Mr. Malbury not find it, he will burn the office down. Search and burn. That has been his order from the beginning."

"What document?"

Phinney ignored the interruption. She snatched all the separate threads of evidence, trying to make sense of them all. "You said Pierre DeChambeaux introduced you to this man Jacques. Jacques—that's an interesting name. You didn't say Jack."

Olivia Stowbridge inhaled sharply. Orion shifted, his boots scraping on the floor.

"Jacques. Jack. Those are very close. The French name is easy to Anglicize. For Pierre to know him, this Jacques must be French. Another *émigré*. Would Pierre continue to work with the man responsible for his son's murder?"

The truth sheeted across her eyes, blinding her. When sight came back, she saw Mrs. Stowbridge, both hands pressed to her face, her eyes wide and teary.

The older woman had said this man Jacques threatened her. *He will inflict ... consequences. He never lets anyone go. He tugged on the leash.* And then she worried about the children's safety. *These men care nothing about innocent children.*

Fear.

Olivia Stowbridge had not said that Boss Malbury was evil. The boss ruled London's criminals. She had merely said that she had *met* Henry Malbury.

This Jacques was not a criminal, then. Not a criminal like the other criminals.

Phinney's mind leapt to *spy*. A man who controlled many. A man who liked tugging on the leashes of those under his power.

A man who feared a document would be found and used against him.

A single spy would not control many. If evidence developed against him, he would run. Only a man who controlled many, who controlled a multi-branched operation would remain and try to wipe out the evidence against him.

Conrad's case. The French spymaster. Jacques—going under the name Jack.

A surname, and the French spymaster would be caught.

"Tell me his name."

"Josephine, no." Deep horror hollowed her voice. "He has guards. Any evidence against him will disappear, be burned to ashes. It always is."

A leash that never was released. Olivia's tension. Orion's scowl. "You need not tell me if it is the man who visited here on the day we arrived. He introduced himself. Jack Salsby."

She paled. Tears trickled down her cheeks.

Jack Salsby. Who had bowed when he met Phinney. When he straightened, he had grinned, and she disliked him from that moment. Why? The sly angle of that grin? The glint in his dark eyes? The way he brushed past her when Orion came to say his coach waited? "What is his French surname?"

"Don't—don't say his name aloud. Don't even think it. You must leave London, Josephine. This instant. You and the children."

"Mr. Titterstone had a file, taken from an office in Liverpool—where Peter had moved his law practice. He sent Richard Malbury to retrieve the file—only Mr. Titterstone wouldn't give it up. Malbury didn't find the file, so it is still there, in the office. I can find it."

"No." She dashed away the tears. "Josephine, you do not understand—he will *kill* you."

"Who works with him? Richard Malbury. Pierre DeChambeaux. Mr. Titterstone—who is no more. Does Mr. Montjoy work with him? I remember that you once mentioned Claude Thierry and Robert LeBrun. Were they part of his French spy ring?"

"What do you know about that?"

"When Peter left London, he probably hoped to sever any connection to French spies. They are spies, aren't they? And they killed Peter rather than risk his telling the authorities. They killed Peter and Rosie.

"Josephine—. He will kill you, too. He will kill the children. He may kill all of us."

"And then he will burn down the mission, because that is what he does. He will burn the mission even though the second floor has beds upon beds of patients who cannot walk. But he wouldn't care about that. He doesn't care who is killed, as long as he is safe. We have to stop him."

"How?"

"I will tell my constable. I will give him that file. I will tell him *Jack Salsby*. It may help to know his real name. Who is he? Jacques Saltz—?"

The older woman sat limply, hands covering her stomach, as if Phinney's determination had sapped her own.

"Olivia," she whispered, "evil works in the shadows. Light makes it retreat. Let us shine a light on this man, and remove the shadows he hides in."

But the older woman didn't respond.

"You need caution," Orion said. He passed her, going around the desk to Olivia. "More than you can be killed. Or he will make you disappear and wish you were in a hole covered with good dirt."

"The children?"

"You be cautious, Miss Josephine. You have answers that you think you need. Now you tell your constable, so he knows to look for your body when you go missing."

"Do you know his name?"

Olivia grasped Orion's hand, pale white inside an ebony grip.

"Jacques Saultsein. You tell your constable, Miss."

"I will," she swore.

But first she would find that file in George Titterstone's office.

Chapter 15

As the soft light of dusk faded, Conrad dashed up the mission steps. Full of his plans to move Phinney and the children, he rapped on the door then crossed his arms to wait.

At the corner, a lamplighter climbed his three-step ladder. Lifting the smudged lamp-post glass, he touched a wick to his lantern and then to the lamp before replacing the glass, climbing down, and whistling on his way. Light warmed the windows of the buildings along the street. For all of its grime, the warm summer evening deepening into night had a magical allure for the country boy that he remained in his heart.

The door opened. Conrad turned to see a boy, a scrawny lad barely the height of the latch. The boy blocked his entrance.

"Yer the constable?"

He put size with dialect. "You must be Vic."

"Talked about me, did she?"

"Only in passing." The boy didn't step back, and Conrad grasped that unanticipated trouble had once more reared its snaky head. "Phinney agreed not to go to her work this evening. Please tell me she didn't.

The pugnacious look vanished. The boy glanced over his shoulder then stepped down from the double entry and onto the porch. He drew the door shut. "She left an hour ago."

"She didn't need to return to that work. I told her I would move you all out of this place tomorrow."

"She's after a file, the one old Titterstone took from an office in Liverpool."

"How do you know this?"

"I picked the locks for the men to get into the office and the desk where it was kept."

Conrad eyed the boy while those snippets of information unwrapped into a larger box than they came from.

Phinney hadn't mentioned that the boy Vic had a criminal trade, one that he must have earned a reputation for in Liverpool. A reputation that got him hired to break into offices. And the boy had seen the men take the file from the office. A file that Phinney wanted. Because Titterstone had wanted it.

He had a dozen questions more to ask, but they would have to wait. "What's in this file that makes Phinney desperate to get it?"

"She thinks it's got clues to the murders of her family."

"Does it?"

The boy shrugged his thin shoulders. His gaze darted along the street, watched, then returned.

Conrad matched this unknown file to Richard Malbury's repeated demand for a document. Titterstone's refusal to produce that unknown document had got him killed.

"What you gonna do?"

Conrad shrugged in his turn. "Did you tell them this?" He bent his head to indicate the mission and the people inside.

"Mrs. Stowbridge calls her *Josephine*."

The *non sequitur* didn't throw Conrad. Obviously raised in rum districts, the boy would parse loyalty very carefully. Even as he accepted Vic's trust, he wondered what kept the boy from offering a similar trust to Mrs. Stowbridge and her loyal servants. "The custodian at the building—."

"Old Gregory," Vic supplied.

"Yes. He turned over his key to Titterstone's office. Phinney won't be able to enter."

"That's crock. She's got a master key. Besides, I taught her how to pick a simple lock."

"Damn," he whispered. "You're staying here?"

"I'm keeping watch on Elise and her brother. You get Phinney." He opened the door and slipped inside.

And Conrad dropped quickly down the steps.

A hackney coach waited at the corner. Conrad hailed the coachman. "Are you for hire? I'm a constable. I must reach Gresham Street quickly."

"I'm waiting on a fare."

"I'll pay double rate."

"Climb up."

"All speed," he advised, and the coachman clucked to the horse, rolling forward before Conrad landed on the seat.

. ~ . ~ . ~ .

Phinney wished Mr. Gregory would go about his business.

She'd surprised both husband and wife with her arrival, "as usual. I do need my pay," she claimed, sticking to her role as Mrs. Coates, war widow with children to support.

"I made sure you wouldn't be here tonight."

"Now, Mrs. Gregory, why would you think that?" She hung her cloak on a peg by the back door and took down the cleaning apron, wrapping the strings and tying them in front.

"Why, you were so shaken up last night," the older woman

declared.

"Those constables," her husband pointed his pipe, "they don't want nobody going in Mr. Titterstone's office."

"Mr. Gregory, if that blood is not scrubbed from the floor, it will stain the wood."

"She's right, Will. That has to be cleaned."

"Then you'll have to do it, wife, for I'll not have Mr. Montjoy vowing we interfered with all those case files. We'll leave those where they are, and Mr. Montjoy can get a clerk to sort the mess. He was most particular that Mr. Titterstone's office be kept secure."

"Mr. Montjoy was here?" Phinney asked, pretending trouble with the apron strings.

"In the afternoon, long after they took Mr. Titterstone's body away. He said he needed a file from Mr. Titterstone's office."

"Did he find it?"

"Now why would you be worritin' 'bout that?"

"No reason. Only it was a right mess, like a whirlwind had been through."

"That reminds me, Mrs. Coates. I'll need back that master key I gave you."

"But I won't be able to get into the offices to clean."

"Now, Will, how's she supposed to do her work?"

"You could switch floors with her, wife."

"And take twice as long! For neither of us will know what's to do. No, Will, we'll do our regular work. When Mrs. Coates has finished, she can clean up down here while I scrub the blood off the floor."

Reaching into the voluminous skirt pocket where she kept the master key, Phinney encountered a folded paper. *What?* Then she remembered the crumpled paper that had missed the waste bin. She had intended to peruse it then had forgotten it after the murder.

She tugged out the key, hoping the Gregorys didn't hear the paper's crackle as loudly as she did. "Will I receive my pay tonight?"

Will Gregory's eyebrows beetled. "On Saturday, as usual."

The Gregorys completely overset Phinney's plan. She had to agree but prayed that an opportunity to enter Mr. Titterstone's office presented itself before the night ended. She gathered her basket and broom and dust bin. He grudgingly agreed to carry the lantern.

She sighed every time Mr. Gregory fumbled to unlock an office door. Since many of them had additional interior rooms with closets, all of those sighs left her a little light-headed. Several times she pointed out missed doors to side rooms then sighed all the louder. When he grumbled at the time she spent in each office, she clanked her broom handle against doors then dropped her dust bin which caused a careful sweep-up of the dust and waste.

He grew impatient before she'd finished the third floor. When she began sweeping the stairs down from the third floor, he protested, "Here now. That can wait until you've finished the offices."

"But this is the order that Mrs. Gregory told me to follow."

He huffed and patted his foot.

She didn't speed up. She even swept the outer edge of the banisters, a task she hadn't previously done. As she came up the stairs, she carefully dusted every banister rail. Then she began the flight to the fourth floor. At the landing, she picked up her basket with its cloths, the broom, and the large dust bin. She had a vague plan to spill it again, but he gruffly said, "Here" and took it from her.

As she started in the anteroom of Mr. Fulbright's office, Mr. Gregory lost patience. "I can't keep nursemaidin' you. I got the coal to deliver. I'm going to unlock all the doors for you, Mrs. Coates, all but the door to Mr. Titterstone's office."

She dampened her jubilation. "Of course, Mr. Gregory. Shall I do that office next, so that you can lock it up first when you come back with the coal?"

"I got the first and second floors to deliver. I'll be lucky if I finish before Mr. Bannockburn arrives. That old cuss is always early." Muttering, he stomped off with that curious quick-step from his smashed knee healed stiff.

Phinney continued to dust Mr. Fulbright's outer office as footsteps and jangling keys faded. She heard the master key scrape open several locks, but the sound faded as Mr. Gregory worked through the more distant offices. She did hear him reach the outer door for *Titterstone & Montjoy, Solicitors*. The lock was stiff, and he grumbled until it turned. His footsteps faded, paused, returned then faded again before returning.

When he found her, she was dusting shelves in the closet of Mr. Fulbright's inner office. "They're all opened now, Mrs. Coates. I remembered every door."

"Thank you, Mr. Gregory."

He stood there, but she whisked her cloth over several files. He turned and stomped out.

When a door banged shut, she reckoned it led to the back stair. She finished the little closet then began Mr. Fulbright's inner office. She skipped the baseboards and windows. She dumped his dust bin into hers, swiped a rag over the obvious surfaces, then packed up and headed for her whole reason for coming tonight.

Phinney held her breath as she crossed the threshold, but no ghost rose to drive her away.

She propped her broom in a corner. Tucked into her bun, well hidden by the mobcap, were the lockpicks that Vic had loaned. She reached for them—but cold gusted over her, as if someone opened a door to a winter wind—or a ghost swept past.

Crouching before Mr. Titterstone's door, new fear landed on her shoulders. She tried to shake off superstition by listening, concentrating hard to hear any distant sound. All was silent. No stomping, no grumbling, no jangling keys.

She would wait a few seconds more. And the crumpled paper in her pocket would be her excuse. She drew it out, unfolded it then smoothed the crumpled creases again. Then she turned the paper to the light cast by her lantern.

It was a portion of a letter—the third page if she believed the number on the top right. She recognized Mr. Titterstone's handwriting. He had stopped in mid-sentence, crossed out a few lines. Then the other writer penned his list. After that, someone wadded up the paper and pitched it to the dust bin. And missed.

A rental agreement, and the lessee in arrears. She wondered who the lessee and lessor were and where the rental property was. She hadn't thought either solicitor concerned themselves with such mundane matters as property leases. Yet they served wealthy clients like Mr. Bennett Parton of Parton March. Perhaps rental agreements were part of their duties.

She tossed the paper into the dust bin. Then she listened again and still heard nothing.

She fumbled for Vic's lockpicks. The first pick went smoothly into the lock. She slid it around, getting a feel for the lock as Vic had instructed, then she inserted the second pick and set to work. The boy swore most locks were simple, "fixed up to send thieves off to easier prey." This lock fit that description, turning easily.

The only problem was that Vic hadn't taught her how to lock the door back.

If she left the door shut, Mr. Gregory might never check it. By dawn she would be gone, never to return. Mr. Gregory would connect her to Olivia Stowbridge and the mission, but she doubted he would pursue her.

Nor would he mention the opened door to Mr. Montjoy, for he would not risk the solicitor's wrath for disobeying orders.

Dawn would see her safe.

She snatched up her cleaning basket and lantern before she entered. And closed the door behind her.

Her gaze skittered past the ledgers and documents on the floor, straight to where Mr. Titterstone had lain. A browning stain circled where his head had been.

Phinney looked away. She set her basket and lantern on the desk. Then she headed for the painting, the Thames River in flood, high waters under the London Bridge. Hope was a physical pang as she lifted it off its nail.

The artist was good, not great. The buildings were slightly out of perspective. The tumultuous storm clouds looked muddy rather than threatening.

Holding her breath, she turned the painting over.

Tucked between the two nails that held the right side of the canvas in the frame was an envelope. She snatched it up. The envelope bore no name or direction. Plain wax had sealed it, but someone—Mr. Titterstone?—had carefully lifted the seal to keep it intact.

Do I dare read it now? No. Mr. Gregory might return. She didn't want to be interrupted when she read this document, so important that Mr. Titterstone had stolen it from an office in Liverpool and hidden it in his office here. And someone else thought the document important and sent Richard Malbury to retrieve it and kill Mr. Titterstone when he refused to give it up.

Into her pocket the envelope went. She patted her skirt over the pocket, ensuring that no bulge would betray her. Then she replaced the painting on its nail, straightened it with the tip of her finger.

Now, to leave.

The outer office door opened.

She froze—then snatched a damp cloth from her basket and slid to the bloodstain. Her back was to the door, but she didn't change position. She dropped down. As her cloth touched the stain, the door opened.

"What are you going here?"

Phinney froze at the voice, the last one she wanted to hear. Her strangled throat managed, "Cleaning, sir."

"Get out."

"I got to finish here, sir."

"Curse you, I told you to get out."

Keeping her chin tucked, she climbed to her feet. She didn't want Richard Malbury to recognize her. She reached for her basket.

"Wait. You were here last night. What did you see?"

The basket was solidly in her hand. "Me, sir? No, sir. I come to work just this night. T'other girl didn't come. Scared of ghosts."

She'd said too much. His sharpened attention was a tangible weight. He stepped between her and the door. "I know you."

"Sir? No, sir."

"Yes. I never forget a pretty face. Yours was in a rose garden."

That old memory startled her into looking up.

"Yes, I do know you. Which means you know me. You can identify me to the local constables."

"No. No, sir. I didn't work here last night."

He grinned. "Keep talking. Every word sharpens the memory.

Especially with all of those 'no's'. Say something else. I almost have the memory."

That memory was the last thing she wanted. The basket had little weight. If she struck him with it, she would only anger him, not escape. But—.

She saw the lantern as he reached for her.

Phinney swung the basket at him. He recoiled. That gave her the inches needed to snatch the lantern. She swung that around. It struck his arm. The metal casing collapsed. The candle, still burning by a strange miracle, spilled to the floor. Onto the documents and the open ledgers. Little flames saw fuel and leaped to feed.

He grabbed her arm. "What have you done?"

The lantern was reduced to the bail and the square plate that formed the top, but she slung it back then over, a roundhouse, Vic had called it. The blow completed the lantern's disintegration.

And Richard Malbury staggered away, clutching his head, blood gushing under his fingers. He swore and reached for her again.

Phinney jumped away. Mindful of the pistol he'd used last night, she fled for the door. She slammed it behind her, slammed the outer door, then picked up her skirts and ran for the front stairs, closer, wider, and better lit.

Chapter 16

Lamplight glinted off long blonde hair streaming behind the running girl. Vic sprinted. He had to catch her before she reached the corner of Kirkgardie Street. Elise didn't hear him behind her. When he grabbed her arm and whirled her around, he discovered why.

Tears streamed down her cheeks. She gulped back sobs. "Let me go!"

"Hush. You want 'em to hear you?"

Her big eyes focused on him. She caught a sob behind her hand.

"Stop crying."

"I can't," Elise wailed her proof.

"You have to. You're a lackwit, coming here by yourself."

Anger stopped her tears, as he'd expected. Her little fist flew, hitting his blocking arm. She was faster, stronger than the last time she'd tried that, in Liverpool. At least she no longer hit like a girl.

"We need to get back to the mission," he added, knowing she would protest which would dry up more tears. With her protest would come the reason she'd ignored the good sense he'd spent all afternoon talking into her.

"We have to get back to the boxes. We have to, Vic. They'll have looked to see where we were. They'll figure it out. And then they'll move all those documents. They might dump them somewhere, like the river. Or burn them. Then we'll never find it. We'll never know the reason they killed my parents!"

"I'll go with you."

"You can't stop—Oh!" She flung her skinny arms around him, and the last particle of his heart that was his own became hers.

When he was certain she'd calmed and no sniffling would betray them, they crept across Kirkgardie to the street behind the warehouse. He spotted two men standing at the warehouse's side entrance. His heart sank. If they had stationed watchmen, getting into the building unnoticed would be impossible.

Then the men parted and walked along the street, heading for the corners of the block.

He hustled Elise into a doorway, crowding her into the corner where the light wouldn't glint off her fair hair. He dragged off his stocking cap. No one would notice his dull brown. He shoved it into her hand. She stared at it blankly then frowned. Twisting her tail of hair, she crammed the stocking cap over her head and hair.

The river burbled beyond the quay, asking them to *Come, look*. The passing watchman never looked around. He clomped along, steps steady as hoofbeats.

A shiny new lock had replaced the rusty one. Vic hesitated. Here was the evidence that the men in charge of the warehouse had figured out how the fire-setting intruders had entered. When he knelt to work on the lock, Elise peered over his shoulder. He didn't know if she noticed the lock's difference.

The tumblers gave way to his picks so easily he wondered if they were oiled slick. When he removed the wires, they had no gunk. As soon as he removed the lock, Elise crowded past. It was his turn to grab her jacket to keep her from barging in. He left the lock on the hasp and closed the door, but the barest glance would reveal that someone had gotten past the lock for the second night.

He crept before her into the warehouse, darkened like last night, with lanterns at the front entrance and along the central walkway and at the top of the stairs.

Smoke hung in the air. Vic kept behind the larger crates.

Footsteps alerted them. They ducked down then crawled forward on hands and knees as the walker neared then passed by.

"More watchmen," she whispered, stating the obvious.

He didn't answer.

Tonight, they had no lantern. He'd thought Elise would have sense enough to bring one, especially since her job last night had been to carry it and use the shutters to hide the light. She'd left without it, a sign of her upset. They would need light once they entered the office. He eyed a lantern on a post, but it didn't have shutters.

This was a mistake. They weren't ready for this. Twice the number of watchmen now guarded the building. The lock had changed. The back of his neck tingled, like a big hand had grabbed it, squeezed hard, then let go.

A man ran past Vic and Elise, hiding near the stairway. Another man came from the far side of the warehouse. They talked so fast, the Cockney so thick he couldn't follow every word. A door slammed at the front.

Vic slipped from behind the crate and scurried up the stairs. Elise came on equally silent feet, her shaky breath the only betraying sound.

Up here the smoke was thicker, the building's great cavern trapping air that never circulated. As he turned toward her pa's office, the hair on his nape lifted. He faltered, and Elise bumped into him. "What?"

"Hsst," and she fell silent.

He knelt and applied his picks. The locks worked smoothly, just like last night. He stared at the lantern hanging from a nail far along the balcony. Then he rose, pocketed his picks.

"What is it?" she hissed. "Oh, a lantern. I forgot."

"We'll manage." He didn't know how.

The door opened at a touch. The smoke smell wafted out, somehow different. They slipped safely inside. He shut the door and leaned against it

Metal clanked as a lantern unshuttered. At the brighter light, Vic winced then saw the man seated across from the door. He smoked a pipe. His legs were splayed to accommodate a bulging belly.

"Good evening. I have been waiting for you."

And he smiled.

Vic jerked open the door. He shoved Elise through—into the grasp of a bearded man. The man picked her up then dropped her back inside. She fell to her knees.

Vic helped her stand. Now, when they faced trouble, she didn't cry. Her hand slipped into his and gripped his fingers tightly.

The belly man puffed on his pipe then removed it. "Now is the time we must talk."

"We got nothing to say."

"Who are you? You are too old to be Henry."

"He's Vic." Elise tried to crowd in front of Vic, but he kept her at his side. "You leave him alone. He's mine!"

"Vic, is it? No doubt you are the one who picked the locks. Vic the lockpick," he mused. "From Liverpool."

He lifted his chin. Elise's cold hand gripped his fingers tighter.

"And the Vic who helped George Titterstone acquire the file that I was certain was lost."

He tried to shrug, but a heavy hand clasped his nape, preventing any movement. He didn't need to answer, though. Belly Man seemed to let his words run like the river.

"I thought you and Mustache—Mr. Titterstone," Elise amended, "worked together."

Belly Man grinned. "Titterstone wanted an association only when it benefitted him. When he no longer saw a benefit, he wanted to slip my leash. I do not work that way. He learned that lesson too late. His partner knows it now."

"Mr. Montjoy," she muttered.

"Indeed, little girl."

"Where is Mr. Montjoy?"

"Bringing the last mouse. Then I will have the whole nest."

"The last mouse? Not Phinney!"

"Josephine Darracott, *exactement.*"

"And Hank?" Vic dared to ask.

"The little boy stays where he is, under the watch of one I trust."

"Mrs. Stowbridge."

"Of course."

Vic struggled, but the grip tightened on his neck. Elise gasped.

"Take them to the office," Belly Man ordered, and Beard dragged them backward. A thin man stood off to the right of the door, holding the lantern, but Vic had no time to see him. Beard hauled them onto the balcony then propelled them toward the stairs.

Who was Belly Man? Was he Boss Malbury, the one every criminal in London ran scared of? Orion had refused to talk about the Boss. Vic hadn't dared to ask a stranger.

Beard kept them stumbling down the stairs then along the aisle. Beyond the smoke, Vic couldn't see any evidence of the fire he'd started last night.

Three men waited at the front. At their approach, one held up a hand. "Side door, sir. Jest like ya thought."

"Nail it shut."

"Need it in case of fire."

"You let another fire start in my warehouse, and you will think those flames better than what you will face from me. Take them into the office. We will wait there for my carriage."

That sounded like a one-way journey. Vic wriggled and struggled, but Beard had a good grip. One man darted past to open the door.

Elise sobbed.

Then Beard shoved them inside, released them as they plunged forward.

Vic caught Elise, and she grabbed his arm to steady herself.

He wanted to demand what would happen next. He wanted to bargain for her life. He said nothing. The cards were stacked against them.

As Belly Man and Lantern came into the office, Vic saw a man seated against the wall. His hand rested on the desk. He had white muttonchop whiskers and a fancy green and purple striped vest. He stood as the boss came in, giving up his chair.

Elise gasped. "*Grandpére*! What are you doing here?"

The old man winced but didn't answer. He turned his head so he wouldn't have to see his granddaughter.

Belly Man chuckled. "*Eh bien, Pierre*. Tell her who you work for."

"Elise, child, you should be in Merrybush."

"Merrybush is in ashes, *Grandpére*. What does he mean? Do you work for him? Have you always worked for him? I thought you worked for a bank or for the government."

Belly Man laughed loudly. "Tell her which government you work for, Pierre."

"I do not think—."

"Tell her." The humor had vanished, replaced by unbending steel.

"I work for the French government," he said to the wall. "Napoleon promised to restore my lands and title."

"But—we're English!"

"You are." He straightened. He still didn't look at her. "I am a Frenchman."

"Then—you are a spy."

He winced. "I am an agent of the French Empire, yes. I do not pretend to be other than I am."

"Did Papa know?" Horror colored her faint voice.

Pierre DeChambeaux didn't answer.

"Your father knew, yes," Belly Man answered, "unfortunately."

"Who are you?" she asked, her voice still small. "He does not have the courage to tell me."

"I am Jack Salsby."

"That is not a French name. I want your real name."

"My apologies, *mademoiselle*." He clicked his heels and bowed. "Jacques Saultsein. Tonight, you will perform a great service for me. By dawn, I will decide if you and your friend—." He paused, eyebrows lifted.

"Vic," he supplied.

"By dawn, I will decide if you and your Vic will serve me best alive or dead."

He expected the old man to protest this threat to his granddaughter, but Pierre DeChambeaux said nothing. He stared at the wall.

And that told Vic, more than anything else, to fear this puppetmaster who hired burglary, arson, and murder done.

.~.~.~.

Phinney flew down the stairs. She slid when she reached the ground floor with its marble tiles. Strong arms caught her before she fell.

"Phinney! Phinney, are you hurt?"

She clutched his sturdy frame. "Malbury!" burst out then "Fire!"

Conrad folded her against him. She heard another man speaking, something about clearing the building, and a quick affirmation followed by running footsteps.

"The Gregorys," she gasped against scratchy blue wool that felt substantial and safe.

"Gibbons will find them. Tell me about the fire."

"I hit him with my lantern. All those papers—. He's bleeding."

"Take her out of here, sir. I'll get Malbury."

She clung when Conrad set her away, but he clasped her hands together and turned her toward a slighter man.

"This is Chief Constable Evans. Go with him, Phinney."

"But—."

"This way, Miss Darracott. My constable knows his business."

"Malbury—he may have a pistol."

"So do I," and Conrad headed away, running up the stairs.

Chief Constable Evans guided her out the front door that she'd never used and to the bricked pavement. "You are unhurt?"

"Yes" although her shaking voice belied her words.

They stood on the pavement, backs to the street, watching the windows of the building, only one on the front façade glowing with a steady light from a fourth-floor room.

Conrad's chief said, "The fire must be out. I see no other lights. For the next couple of hours, Miss Darracott, my constables will be concerned with Richard Malbury's arrest. You would not long endure sitting on a bench in a back hallway of our Constabulary. I believe the best course for you would be to send you home."

"No. I want to stay. Conrad—."

"As I said, Hoppock will be focused on this arrest for a couple of hours, at the minimum. After that, I will release him to you. I promise."

The smile he gave was assuring, friendly, amused. If the light were sufficient, she was certain his eyes would be twinkling. Phinney forced her mind to work more rapidly than her emotions. "I do not wish to interfere with Conrad's duties."

"Shall I admit that he will be distracted until he is assured of your safety? Here is a carriage, most fortuitously. Let me commandeer it for you." He flagged the coachman.

Phinney didn't hear their conversation. After that exchange, Chief Evans stepped to the coach box. He opened the door and conferred briefly before motioning to her.

"Miss Darracott, this gentleman has agreed to take you to your home."

She stared at the building, wondering what Conrad faced with Malbury. Hours waiting. And an envelope burning a hole in her skirt pocket, waiting to be read. She turned and walked to the carriage. *Should I share this document with Chief Evans?* No. Elise should see it first. Phinney would give it to Conrad when he came.

Evans had flipped down the box step of the coach. "This is Sir Henry Morgan," he said before he steadied her climb into the coach. "Miss Josephine Darracott, sir."

A grunt came from the recesses of the forward-facing seat. Phinney settled onto the opposing bench as Evans shut the box door and flipped up the step. She heard him give the address to the mission. The coach lurched as it rolled forward.

"I thank you, Sir Henry," she said clearly, determined to be polite.

The tremor had left her voice, helped on its way by the humor she found in receiving help from a man with the name of England's famous pirate of over a hundred year before.

Another grunt was her answer. A flash of light in the dark box startled her. Then came a double rap on the ceiling of the box, and she realized the flash was light reflecting off the silvered head of Sir Henry's cane, used to signal the coachman. The coach was gaining speed. She clung to the bench.

"We will not travel far," Sir Henry said.

"It is not a great distance," she replied. His voice sounded familiar, yet she couldn't place it. She wouldn't be so presumptuous as to claim an acquaintance, but she could swear they had met.

The coach slowed for a turn onto a main thoroughfare then again picked up speed. The passing lamp posts helped her identify the buildings although they cast little light into the coach box.

When the coach turned again, long before Phinney expected, she leaned toward the window, the better to identify the street. "I am not certain—. I do believe your coachman has taken a wrong turn."

"I would disagree, Miss Darracott. He knows exactly where he is to go."

Sir Henry's voice had changed, casting off the deep grumble and becoming more recognizable. Surprise landed her against the back of her seat.

"Fate is remarkable, isn't it?" Kennedy Montjoy remarked. "I am sent to fetch Miss Josephine Darracott, masquerading as a cleaning maid in my office, no doubt to find evidence to use against my partner and me, and the chief constable in charge of the case hands her into my carriage. May I ask what occasioned his appearance at my building?"

She stared at the passing street. The carriage wasn't flying. Two horses could certainly turn to speed, but at this pace, she wouldn't hurt herself too much when she leaped from the box.

"Stop," he ordered, and she knew he'd seen her hand sneaking for the door latch. "I have a pistol aimed at you, Miss Darracott. I would prefer not to have blood spattered all over my carriage, but I will not hesitate to shoot. Unlike my late partner, I do not hesitate to take any bloody action necessary."

"Does that include ordering the deaths of my sister and my brother-in-law?"

"A tigress! Is that what motivates you?"

She didn't answer.

He remained in the deepest shadows, but the occasional glint of light revealed that he did have something brightly metallic pointed at her.

She watched the passing lamp posts. The streets seemed deserted.

No one would come to her aid. "Where are you taking me?"

"Your presence is requested by the man most concerned by your ... shall we call it an *attempt* to spy in my office? He is looking forward to meeting this little spy causing trouble for him."

"I wasn't spying. I was searching."

"For evidence. About Peter DeChambeaux's death."

"And my sister's!"

"Content yourself, Miss Darracott. Very soon you will have the answers you seek. Then we shall see what he intended to do with you."

"Who is he?" When he didn't answer, she added, "Is Richard Malbury his minion, just as you are?"

"Malbury is. I wouldn't call myself a minion."

"Is this about French spies?"

"Save your questions. Do nothing foolish, and you may see your little imps."

"My imps? Are you talking about the children?"

"A boy and girl."

"No. They are safe in their beds."

"No. They chose to return to the warehouse."

He could have said nothing else that would prove his words—and guarantee that Phinney would make no further attempt to escape.

Chapter 17

Conrad slowed as he approached the open door to the offices of Titterstone and Montjoy.

Smoke hung, heavy and choking, but the light was steady, not the chancy flicker of open flames.

Coughing from the inner office masked his entrance into the anteroom, and the swearing that followed covered his last few steps. "Dammit. I knew she had it. I should have strangled her when I had the chance." A book flew through the doorway and thudded to the floor.

Conrad stepped into the doorway then past it.

Squatting beside the desk, Malbury spotted him and flung a handful of papers. They scattered and fell harmlessly. He laughed, a manic edge removing all humor. Blood streamed from a cut on his brow. "Give me a ledger," and he reached for a thick book laying open on the floor.

Conrad leapt. He knocked Malbury flat. Hauling back for a punch, he realized the man lay still, eyes rolled back and arms flung out. The man groaned and rolled his head sideways.

He reached for the rope twist he used for grips, tucked into his left pocket.

And Malbury surged up, grabbing Conrad's coat while he aimed a punch.

Conrad scrambled back. More papers followed him, then the heavy ledger. As he dodged, Malbury shoved to his feet. He staggered a step then kicked out. His shoe glanced off Conrad's shoulder. He followed with a two-handed blow that would have floored Conrad if the kick had landed.

Then he ran.

Cursing himself, Conrad slipped on the scattered papers. From the outer office came a thud, a louder thump, and more cursing.

He caught Malbury by the shoulder as he heaved up from the floor. "Not so fast." He clipped him hard on the ear. Malbury yelped. He threw a wild punch and drove in behind with a better one. He landed several more punches to Conrad's unprotected ribs.

Conrad got his own punches in. Blood gushed from the nobleman's cut temple and soon from his nose, his face becoming a gory mask. They grappled, the younger man's skill a match for Conrad's strength and dirty tricks gleaned in his nine years on London's streets. He hooked his heel behind the slighter man's and shoved.

Malbury staggered over a chair then tripped. Conrad caught a flailing forearm, twisted it around to spin him then pushed it high up Malbury's back. He forced him to bend forward. And it was done, both of Malbury's hands caught behind his back, held high on the edge of pain. When Conrad compelled him forward, the younger man stumbled out into the main hall and toward the stairs.

Timothy Gibbons met them on the flight between the first and second floors. "You got `im!" Excitement stole his H's.

Malbury slowed, but Conrad kept pushing, and they passed the young constable.

"There was a fire in the open office on the fourth floor. Be certain it's out, Gibbons. Is the building clear?"

"Aye, sir. No one else inside. The chief's waiting."

As he propelled his captive to Chief Constable Evans, Conrad didn't try to hide his satisfied grin.

The chief stared at the blood still streaming from Malbury's temple and nose. "Not quite the condition I expected, Hoppock."

"Only the nose is mine, sir. Phinney did his brow for him."

"That will likely scar," he noted, a lack of concern keeping his tone bland.

Malbury glared.

In the quiet, Conrad heard rumbling wheels and clipclop hoofbeats. "Where is Phinney?"

"Miss Darracott is well on her way to her home."

Malbury straightened his spine. "Darracott? Phinney? Josephine Darracott?" He twisted, a futile attempt to shake off Conrad's grip. "I knew that I recognized her! That bit—."

Conrad cuffed his ear. "Shut up."

"She's a menace! Skinny know-it-all."

"Mr. Malbury, if you are so inclined to talk," the chief sounded calm, but he no longer stood with hands clasped behind him. They hung loose at his sides, ready if needed—although Conrad didn't intend to lose his grip, "then you can tell us the reason you killed George Titterstone."

He snarled. "That's a reason you'll never learn."

"Did he have incriminating information about your French friends? Do not look so surprised, Mr. Malbury. We know that you remain linked to Napoleon's agents here in England. You are even beholden to them, especially to the spymaster. We are most interested in him."

"I will say nothing!"

"I can pry it out of him, sir."

"I'll help," Gibbons added, coming up on the left. "No fire," he added at Conrad's raised eyebrows. "Office is a mess. Gord! `e's like to `ave two black eyes."

"You'll not touch me! You won't dare! My father is a peer of the realm. Before this month is out, I will inherit his title and lands and wealth. His friends in White Hall will support me. All of his friends will! Nothing you charge me with will stick. Never! When I tell them the indignities you have visited upon me, when they see me bleeding and bruised, you will lose your position! All of you!"

"That is interesting." Evans remained bland although he did back a step away from Malbury's spitted words. "How do you know your father will die before the end of the month? Especially since word came this very afternoon that he is rallying under the care of his new physician."

"New physician?" The younger man's stillness warned Conrad to tighten his grip. "What new physician? Where's Dr. Oliver?"

"Rembrandt Oliver has decided that he should return to the Continent. I believe my questions of him two days ago hastened his departure."

"You dog!"

Evans smiled. "That's mild compared to your mother's reaction. By the way, she fled with Oliver. Ah, there's our police wagon, just in time to take our prisoner to gaol. Gibbons, ensure that Mr. Malbury doesn't trip climbing into the box. He's suffered sufficient indignities."

"Aye, Chief." The young constable clipped a salute then took over Conrad's grip, an easy transfer that proved his growing experience in arresting criminals.

Evans watched Gibbons coerce Malbury toward the approaching police wagon, its weathered boards looking grey in the lamplight. "This night will be a long one for Mr. Malbury. And for me. However, Hoppock, you have a young lady who needs your attention."

"Sir, my job is certainly *not* ended. Malbury has to be questioned. He knows the spymaster. He must."

"We have five men here, besides myself and that eager cub. The next couple of hours will see Malbury gaoled, then the boring work begins. We'll need clear official records. I appreciate his warning about interference from White Hall and the House of the Lords. Their interest will be a sticking point if we don't have every jot and tittle marked. I wasn't here in London when they arrested Robert LeBrun and Claude Thierry, but I heard enough of the questions raised and obstacles erected to know Malbury's arrest and charge will also receive extraordinary scrutiny. Incomplete documentation is part of the reason Thierry still sits in his cell rather than hanged alongside LeBrun. Your full attention is necessary, Hoppock, and I know you will be distracted until you assure yourself that Miss Darracott is safely home. Besides, she was still trembling when I put her in a passing hack."

"You put her into a passing hack? Alone?"

"Be calm, Hoppock. She had the reassuring company of an old

gentleman, Sir Henry Morgan. He was happy to play knight gallant to a damsel in distress. Now, off with you. I expect your full attention in the morning. Sharply at 10, Hoppock."

"Sir. Thank you, sir." He snapped a salute as clipped as Timothy Gibbons.

. ~ . ~ . ~ .

A coach waited at the steps of the mission. Standing on the porch was a cloaked woman. She gestured in broad sweeps as she argued with the colossal African. Conrad broke into a run.

Before he reached the pavement, the cloak hood fell back. Lamplight gleamed on golden hair. Not Phinney's dark tresses. Even as he slowed, the African gripped the woman's arm. She struggled to pry off his hand.

"Let me go! They are in danger!"

They didn't refer to Phinney. When Conrad bounded up the steps, the African released her and imposed himself between.

He stopped abruptly, aware he'd read the situation wrongly. "Mrs. Stowbridge," he hazarded since he'd never met the woman, "what's the to-do?"

"The children are missing!"

"The children?"

"Elise and Vic." She pushed at the man, but he didn't budge. "They aren't anywhere in the house. We have looked. Hank said Vic told him to stay with Mhambi. And Orion found the door off its latch."

"Phinney—. Where—where is Miss Darracott?"

"She has not returned. Move, Orion. Are you Mr. Hoppock? Constable Hoppock?"

"He is," the African said. "He is the constable who interviewed her."

"You must help us find the children, Constable!"

"Phinney should be here." He couldn't understand why she wasn't. Even in a slow coach, she would have arrived some time ago.

"She is *not!* She cleans—."

"No. I sent her home from there, long before I left myself. She took a hack. With Sir Henry Morgan."

"That name—. They have used that name before!" Her hands flew to cover her mouth.

The African turned to her. "We will go," he said. "Both of us. You will not go there alone, never again."

Her hands fell from her mouth to grip his arm. Then she turned her intense stare on Conrad. "Josephine is very likely in the same place that the children are."

"The warehouse on Kirkgardie Street," the man offered when Conrad drew a blank.

"Originally, yes. We cannot stand about. He'll have taken them." She pushed past and flowed down the steps, the dark cloak billowing with her speed. "Orion," she didn't look around, but he was a mere step behind her. "Go up with the coachman. Prepare the muskets. I have my pistols. Do you have yours?"

He answered softly, more than a single word, as he opened the coach door. Even though Conrad was barely three steps behind them, he didn't hear what the man said. Then Orion lifted the petite woman inside the box. He didn't wait for Conrad but climbed up the box and settled onto the bench with the coachman. As soon as Conrad slammed the box door, the coach started with a jerk and quickly gained speed.

"Are you armed?" she asked, her attention on the passing buildings.

"I am." The coach didn't turn toward the river. "Where are we heading? Not Kirkgardie and the warehouse?"

"No. He'll not have them there. He can be interrupted there. He'll have taken them to his residence where he can take his time."

"Who, ma'am?"

"Jack Salsby." A bitter name that she spat, as if it fouled her mouth. The passing lamplight flickered on her face. "His real name is Jacques Saultsein. Since his arrival here in England, he has controlled every agent working for Napoleon, including Claude Thierry and Robert LeBrun and Richard Malbury. And his hooks were dug deep into George Titterstone and Kennedy Montjoy."

"And you, ma'am?"

"To my shame, yes," and in the long minutes of the drive through empty London streets, she confessed her involvement with a man she called evil.

Chapter 18

They left the carriage two streets over and walked. Saultsein's house was a detached terrace in the Adams style. In daylight, the white-painted residence would have a view of a pocket park. Roads streamed on either side of the narrow house. Iron-spiked railings kept anyone from venturing off the pavement and into the thick shrubbery that created a second, thornier barricade.

In his dark clothes, Orion was one with the night. He faded away from them when they reached the block, heading for the garden and carriage house that shared a back wall with another residence's garden, the house itself facing the other direction and another pocket park.

Conrad and Olivia Stowbridge turned for the front entrance, lighted by lamps that topped the iron posts supporting the gate. More iron posts at the entry lighted the steps to the front door.

"No lights inside," he whispered although no one was about to hear them.

She touched a finger to her lips then pointed up. "Third window on the first floor."

A crack of light peeped out that sole window.

"He lives in the night. He is always awake at night. It is his time."

"No guards."

"They are inside, so they will attract no attention. Two guard the entrance. Another upstairs. More waiting out of sight."

"This place is too open. Surely a neighbor would notice when several people arrive, especially people who struggled against the guards."

"He may have brought them through the tunnel. Oh yes, there is an old tunnel. It runs underneath the street. A drain to the river. We are not that far from the Thames. Did you not realize?"

He hadn't. A house that looked innocent although guards stood vigilant. A tunnel under the street. No wonder they'd never found clues about the French spymaster's base in London. An increase of visitors wouldn't be noticed, for they would come under cover of darkness or by the tunnel. The guards kept the interior safe while the spiny barberry and iron railings formed a defensive moat. With the thick-walled house detached from the others, the streets creating a noise barrier, Jacques Saultsein had the perfect location for his rings of French agents and for easy disposal of anyone who interfered in his work for Napoleon.

"How are we going to get inside?"

"Fear not, Constable. I have a plan," and she boldly crossed the street.

Conrad followed. He didn't know what else to do.

The gate opened smoothly, silently, yet before they reached the porch, one of the curtains covering the windows beside the door had twitched.

"He moved to his house two years ago," she said conversationally, "after a long search."

They mounted the steps together. The door opened before Conrad lifted his hand to the brass knocker.

And Olivia Stowbridge proved her long connection with the French spymaster when she addressed the stub-haired man who opened the door. "Fultenoy. I have brought a man to meet with Mr. Salsby. Please inform him."

The man eyed Conrad. His twisted mouth and wrinkled face should have identified him, but Conrad remembered no reports with that description. Fultenoy admitted them. "Wait here." He climbed the stair clinging to a paneled wall. The upper stairs curved in a flight across the entrance before continuing upward and upward.

Two beefy men stood on either side of the entrance with its blank walls and uncarpeted floor. A slender footman appeared. Conrad handed over his narrow-brimmed hat then helped Mrs. Stowbridge with her cloak. Standing so close to her, he felt a heavy bump against his leg. The weight of it was too light for a long-bore pistol. That weapon must be dragging down the large reticule that she had brought with her from the carriage. Conrad hadn't noticed it until she turned to accept his help with her cloak.

They didn't speak as they waited. He didn't want to stare at the guards, so he stared at the floor, at the stairs, at a lighter patch on the wall where a painting had recently been removed, with occasional peeks at Mrs. Stowbridge. She intrigued him. He had formed an impression of a benevolent matron running a mission for wounded veterans. The complacent matron that he'd envisioned wasn't this woman who'd told a shivering story of evil and who walked calmly into danger, with weapons at the ready.

She hadn't dressed for her encounter with the Frenchman who'd once been her protector. She wore a simple cotton in heavy grey. Her blonde hair was dressed simply, but she held herself tall, as if she descended into a ballroom in rich silks with jewels adorning her.

A man came to the head of the first flight of stairs. Fultenoy. Behind him came an older man with gunmetal hair, wearing a double-breasted jacket that strained over his round belly. He stopped at the top of the stairs and rested a hand on the banister. "Olivia, my dear, what brings you to me on such a night?"

His command of English gave no hint of French.

"I have brought a friend." She lifted a pale hand to indicate Conrad. He saw it tremble. "You must meet him."

"I am currently involved in important business. Who is he?"

"Part of this."

His trimmed eyebrows rose. "Indeed? Do come up, then. We will be quite a merry crowd."

The ground floor guards didn't move. Their master returned along the hall. Fultenoy waited. He bowed when Mrs. Stowbridge gained the first floor. "Ma'am. You know the procedure."

"Of course. My friend first, though." She stepped away from the stair, forcing the man to shift away from the abbreviated balcony and toward the hall down which Jacques Saultsein had disappeared. "Mr. Hoppock, please raise your arms. Fultenoy will search for a weapon."

He had followed meekly, but at this he gaped. With all her talk of evil, he had not expected her to acquiesce so easily to any search that would discover their weapons.

"Sir," the man said.

"Very well." He didn't know what to do. He faced the stairs then lifted his arms, extending them wide. The man came close behind him. He began by patting Conrad's shoulders then his upper back. When he felt along his forearms, focusing on his wrists and cuffs, Conrad realized he was searching for knives. A man could have sheaths strapped to his arms as well as his upper back, easily accessible.

He turned Conrad's hand, revealing scrapes from the earlier fight with Malbury. "You engaged in fisticuffs this evening, sir?"

"I did." He offered no explanation.

"Unbutton your coat, sir."

Conrad lowered his arms.

"Keep one arm up, sir. Your right, please. Use one hand only to unbutton the coat."

"My apologies." Intent on maintaining the guise Olivia Stowbridge had presented, he managed to keep grit out of the two words, but he wanted to punch the man.

Hands slipped under his coat and patted around, working to the small of his back.

Then the hands were gone. A soft sound caused Conrad to look over his shoulder.

To see Orion carrying Fultenoy into the unlit hallway from which he must have come.

He glanced below. The guards hadn't moved. They hadn't looked up. They had heard nothing.

"Thank you, Fultenoy," Mrs. Stowbridge said to the unconscious man disappearing into the shadows.

In a bare second, Orion emerged, walking soundlessly for a giant. He held a lethal pistol in each hand which reminded Conrad to tug his own pistol out of his capacious pocket.

"Is it still the third door?" she pretended to ask. "I will show myself in, shall I, Fultenoy? Come along, Mr. Hoppock."

He followed again, with Orion behind him.

She'd taken the long-bore pistol from her reticule and handed it to Conrad. From her skirt pocket she brought forth a smaller pistol, silver-tooled, a single-shot. She paused before a door with light streaming from underneath. Memory flashed of opening a door in a dark hallway, and flames erupting over both MacBride and him, like a dragon's breath spewing its hatred. The flames on the other side of this door wouldn't be real but would still be dangerous.

Mrs. Stowbridge tucked her little pistol in the folds of her skirts. With a glance at him and Orion, she opened the door.

The white-paneled room had a gold carpet and honey-colored furniture. Then Conrad saw Kennedy Montjoy turn toward the door. The man's eyes widened.

Olivia Stowbridge swept past him. "Jack," she said. "I want you to meet—."

"Conrad!" Phinney cried. "No!"

Then he was in the room, aiming one pistol at the gaping Montjoy and the other at an older man with silver side whiskers. Only then did he look for Phinney. She knelt near the empty hearth. She clasped a blonde-haired girl to her. A boy with lifted fists stood between them and Jack Salsby.

And the Stowbridge woman aimed her one-shot pistol. Before Salsby could speak, she put a bullet in his left eye.

"Trouble's coming behind you, Constable," the African said, but it was the feet pounding up the stairs that reminded him of the guards. Orion fired a shot down the hall. A man yowled, and the advance stopped. "Take my place," he said and began pulling powder and shot from a pocket.

Conrad took the door. He risked a glance down the hall. Backlit by light and the white-paneled walls of the entrance, a shadow rose from the floor. He fired a shot and wished he knew what was going on behind him.

"Need a pistol?"

"No," he said and handed his pistol for re-loading. He aimed Mrs. Stowbridge's long-bore down the hall. He could hear the guards talking, one man moaning, and decided to try logic. "Your master Jack Salsby is dead."

Two men rushed up the steps. As he aimed, one of them fired. The bullet hit the jamb, and splinters flew. Conrad ducked—and over his head a pistol fired. Orion, holding the line.

"We see you; we shoot you," Conrad warned. "Get out now!"

More muttering, then "How do we know Master Salsby's dead?"

Orion handed a pistol to Conrad, restoring him to two loaded weapons. He strode over to the dead man. Conrad risked a glance to check on Phinney. She and the children were still by the fire. Mrs. Stowbridge stood with them, another pistol in her hand, aimed at the lawyer and the whiskered man.

Orion hoisted up the dead man. The white-whiskered man choked and turned away. Conrad shifted out of the way when Orion neared.

"Here is your master," he shouted as Orion heaved the body through the doorway.

Salsby landed on his back. His legs didn't cross the threshold, but the light from the room clearly illuminated his mutilated face.

"Believe us now?" Conrad shouted.

Their decision came rapidly. "We're gone." They thumped down the stairs, two sets rapid, one halting.

"No!" Montjoy shouted. "Don't leave. It's only the two of them."

"Please sit, Mr. Montjoy," Mrs. Stowbridge said, "or you will soon join Jacques Saultsein in Hell. Orion."

The giant slipped into the hall, moving as silently as when he'd surprised Fultenoy.

Conrad risked another glance into the room.

Phinney had stood. She held her niece in her arms, the girl clinging with arms and legs. Vic had acquired a pistol. With Olivia Stowbridge, he kept watch on the two men.

He wrote out the next fifteen minutes in his report, step by step, but the memory was hazy, as if he witnessed it, not lived and breathed it.

The rope twist he had intended for Richard Malbury came to good use on Kennedy Montjoy. Orion supplied his own rope twist for the whiskered man, whom Conrad learned was Pierre DeChambeaux, the children's grandfather.

Orion ensured the house was empty then dragged Salsby's body well into the hall before they left the room.

While Orion searched the house, Olivia Stowbridge uncovered a cache of documents, tied them with a gold cord cut from the brocade draperies, and gave it to Conrad, proof of Jacques' most recent actions for the French.

Then they trooped downstairs and out of the house. He kept the documents in one hand and Montjoy's shoulder in the other. Like a defeated prisoner on his way to execution, DeChambeaux trudged forward, followed by Vic, careful with the pistol that looked too big for him.

The carriage waited at the gate. The boy clambered up to join the coachman, and then the girl begged to join her friend. When Phinney hesitated, Mrs. Stowbridge said, "Better than sitting in the box watching us keep our pistols on these two."

Montjoy and DeChambeaux climbed awkwardly into the box. Orion followed, pinning them against the box wall with his shoulders. Hands pinned behind them, their ride would be painful. Phinney sat between Conrad and Olivia Stowbridge—who carefully outlined for Conrad what he would say and what he wouldn't say.

Orion was not to be mentioned.

Jacques Saultsein had had a pistol with which he threatened the children.

And Conrad had fired the killing shot.

"I'm not that good of a shot," he protested.

"Desperation steadied your aim."

"Those two," he indicated their two prisoners, "will tell a different story."

"Mr. Montjoy is aware that his wife and children are totally unprotected. Aren't you, sir? *M'sieur* DeChambeaux has caused enough grief for his grandchildren, haven't you, sir?"

The old man nodded, or the motion could have been the carriage rocking his downbent head.

Montjoy stared wide-eyed at the petite woman who calmly dictated their story. "You wouldn't dare hurt my children."

"Mr. Montjoy, you know my years with Jacques. The best lesson he taught was how to be ruthless. You have only one little thing you must remember. Constable Hoppock fired the shot that killed him."

"And what do I get?"

"Lawyers. Always bargaining." She sighed. "Do you truly wish to bargain for your children's continued safety?"

Conrad didn't trust Montjoy's crumbling agreement. His chief would know the truth, for he wouldn't lie. Evans spotted lies too easily. The official record, though, would be neatly tied up with the two omissions that Mrs. Stowbridge demanded.

As they reached the Constabulary, pink tinged the clouds packing in from the east. Orion climbed out first, to check the street then watch their prisoners descend.

Phinney clung to Conrad when he would have climbed out. "Conrad Hoppock, I don't want—please—after tonight—."

He took her hand from his arm and dropped a kiss to her work-roughed fingertips and then to her palm. "I have to report, and these documents have to go to the right person." He indicated the packet on his knees. "But I will come to you, Josephine Elizabeth Darracott, before the sun sets on this day. I promise."

"You had better, Constable Hoppock." Then she dashed her hand across her eyes and leaned back into the shadows of the coach.

Orion followed Conrad up the steps and into the Constabulary, lagging behind in order to push Montjoy and DeChambeaux to the desk.

The constable on duty looked up, then a shout came from down the hall. "'oppock! Two of 'em! Gord! Where's Salsby? Chief, Chief, 'oppock is back."

When the ensuing chaos ebbed, with Montjoy and DeChambeaux escorted to holding cells and his chief congratulating him on surviving the gunfire "although Salsby's death is regrettable", Conrad realized that Orion had slipped away.

The coach had also left.

Chapter 19

"Tell me again about Mrs. Stowbridge shooting that man."

Elise gagged. "Please don't. I can still see it too clearly."

Vic looked over her bent head and gave a jerk of his head. Hank nodded, understanding the signal, but he didn't let his sister wiggle too far from the memory. "I guess your death skill isn't going to be shooting, is it?"

"No. Vic can have that."

"What then?" the boy persisted. He tore off a quarter of the flatbread that he'd brought from the kitchen and offered it to Elise. She shuddered and pushed his hand away, so he reached it around her to Vic. "What will you pick for your death skill? You got to have one. And you got to practice it, so you can use it when it's time, without thinking."

With the late summer sun warming them and birds twittering and flitting in the strip of garden, Vic found it hard to think of *death skills*. He found it harder yet to remember last night. It could have been a nightmare—only he had bruises on his neck from where the guard squeezed hard to control him.

"*Have* to have. *Have* to practice," Elise corrected, sounding like her aunt.

Vic considered Hank's words. The boy was repeating Mhambi. When they'd arrived this morning, she and her many kitchen knives had stood watch over the little boy sleeping in the front room. Once she saw Orion and Mrs. Stowbridge, she gave a nod and returned to her domain. Wonderful aromas soon filled the house as she prepared her version of a breakfast worthy of heroes.

The cook's talk of a life skill and a death skill fascinated Hank. Maybe because it was good sense, especially after last night, when Vic realized that he didn't know how to fire the pistol Mrs. Stowbridge had given him. He'd watched Orion speedily re-load two pistols and felt little more than useless.

Mhambi was right, too, about the practice. His own experience, learning to pick locks, had a lot of frustration before success. Since people were constantly coming up with new kinds of locks, he would be constantly learning how to pick them.

That was his life skill. Soon, he needed to learn his death skill.

Although knowing how to shoot a pistol hadn't saved Jack Salsby.

Hank whipped out a penknife and threw it. The tiny blade buried in a knot of wood. "That's what I'm learning from Mhambi. She says in this house, you got—*have* to have life and death skills. This is my death skill."

"And your life skill?" Vic asked.

"I haven't worked that out yet. Did you know Mhambi's name means *traveler*? That's in Zulu. She picked that name for herself when Mrs. Stowbridge freed them. They didn't want to keep the names given them when they were sold. New life, new name. That's what Mhambi says." The words kept pouring out of Hank, evidence of how much he'd gleaned during his time in the kitchen. "Liyana says her name means *it's raining* in Zulu, and she can rain death with her poisons. Mhambi laughed when she said that, so I'm not certain that's right."

"What's Zulu?" Vic asked in spite of himself.

"That's their tribe."

Elise roused. "Orion is not a Zulu name. It's from Greek mythology. And it's a constellation of stars. The hunter. He should pick his own name."

"His *own* name is a big long thing that starts off like Orion. Besides, Mhambi says he likes Orion for a name." He jumped off the steps and retrieved his penknife then threw it again, farther away. "You need a good death skill," he told his sister then ran to fetch it. "Something really dangerous, like knives."

"Poison," she said. "Liyana can teach me."

"Are you going to be bloodthirsty assassins, then?" rumbled Orion, coming behind them without warning.

Vic turned, never liking someone at his back.

Hank grinned at the giant. "Mhambi says you need a life skill and a death skill. She cooks and throws knives. She's going to teach me."

"Both of them, young master?"

"Why not? I just decided. Nobody else cooks like Mhambi. I want to learn how she knows which spices to use and how long to cook meat and beans and—." He held up the flatbread. "And keep my belly full with this."

Orion's white teeth flashed. "Good choices. And you, Master Vic? What life and death skills have you picked?"

He started to answer, but his gut changed the words to a question. "What's yours?"

"I am a hunter."

Vic considered the African, tall and lean, strong and sturdy, moving silently, acting quickly. Hunter. Life and death both. "Would you train me?"

"The hunt of the city is not the hunt of the savanna."

He didn't know what a savanna was, but he understood what Orion meant. "I know."

"Very well. And you, young miss?"

"She's going to learn poisons," Hank supplied when she hesitated, "from Liyana."

"The lore of the plant is more than death. It contains life and healing. Life is a harder lesson than death."

Elise straightened. She met Orion's gaze then turned to look at the green garden, washed clean by the morning's rain. "Healing. I will learn that, too. Yes. Life and death in one skill. Like hunting."

He dipped his head. "Good. Now. Two men have come to speak with Miss Josephine, but Mrs. Stowbridge thinks you should attend this meeting as well."

"Scoping out the enemy?" Hank asked.

"Knowing the other predators is an important skill."

They followed Orion into the house, the interior hall overly dark until their eyes adjusted.

The meeting was in Mrs. Stowbridge's office. Like a serene queen holding court, she sat behind her great desk. Vic would never again look at her without remembering her expressionless face, before *and* after she pulled the trigger that killed Jack Salsby.

Two men sat in chairs before the desk. They had turned when the door opened, but seeing only the tall African and three children, they returned to their conversation with Mrs. Stowbridge, as if the new entrants were unimportant. And Vic made another decision: he would always remember that danger came in many forms, including from the young and supposedly helpless.

The children crowded onto the bench of the recessed window. Orion took a straight-backed chair beside the door, leaving for Phinney the cushioned chair with its stitched flowers on the back.

The mantel clock ticked loudly while they talked of the wounded men healed in the mission when the military hospital would have left them to waste.

Then came footsteps, light and hurried.

The men rose and faced the door. Orion reached into his coat pocket. Hank fingered his penknife. Mrs. Stowbridge had her hands under the desk. Vic remembered that single shot with her pistol and feared her the most.

Phinney came in. The two men bowed deeply.

And the room's tension ebbed.

"Miss Darracott? Miss Josephine Darracott? I am Sir Roger Nazenby." The older man, all in grey except for a sun-bright yellow tie, lifted a monocle and examined her through it. "This is my colleague, Lord Giles Hargreaves. Your nation owes you a great debt of gratitude."

She stopped, flustered, then lowered herself into the chair. One hand clung to the seat, as if she needed to hold to something. "Sirs, I— am honored by your statement, but I did not act alone. Mrs. Stowbridge, Orion here, Constable Hoppock, and these children, all of us had an equal part in whatever it is you think we have done."

Good for Phinney, Vic smirked, *refusing to claim all the glory*. Elise nudged him, and Hank beamed, the only one with unearned glory.

"Miss Darracott, your humility is commendable, but—." She grimaced. Sir Roger stopped. Fingering the gold-cased monocle, he turned to the younger man whose dark clothing was not designed to attract attention. Vic liked him for that alone. "Hargreaves, perhaps … ."

"Yes, sir. Miss Darracott. Mrs. Stowbridge." He turned a little to include the older woman then sent a smile to the children and to Orion. "Let us begin once more. Forgive our fulsome compliments. They are indeed heartfelt. You must understand that you have accomplished something that Sir Roger and myself have worked to achieve. I have assisted him since '11, but I know he has invested over two decades of his life to the destruction of several circles of French spies operating in Britain. We have had successes, but never did we locate the spider at the center of his vast web. You have not only located him and handed us evidence as proof, but you have also removed him before he could escape. Your country owes you a great debt."

"Sirs. Your—you—I must confess that our motives going into this—." Phinney looked confused then said in a quick rush, "Well, this had little to do with higher ideals like patriotism. Frankly, my lord, I wanted justice for my sister's death. Justice is very close to revenge, I must admit. So you see, any gratitude is misnamed."

"If I may, Miss Darracott," this was the older man, no longer tongue-tied by compliments, "your motives matter not one whit in the balance against the service you have performed."

Vic nudged Elise who nudged Hank. They might get medals for this.

"Sir Roger the spycatcher?"

That was Mrs. Stowbridge, as expressionless as last night.

He lifted his monocle to examine her. "An accolade that I should no longer bear after the work you all achieved last night, ma'am."

"We did very little," that was Phinney, "except get ourselves into danger."

"You also worked yourselves out of that danger. Chief Constable Evans informed us early this morning of last night's events. And the events of the previous days. We have had but a cursory look at the documents brought in by Constable Hoppock, at your behest, ma'am, as he tells me. That list of names and locations and events will keep us busy for some time. I do believe Napoleon's network of spies in Britain is now destroyed. If my praise seems too effusive, it is only because I have had so many frustrations and disappointments in accomplishing that very task."

"We are limited in the information we can share with you," Hargreaves inserted. "Much of our work covers multiple years, on-going events, and several people who hold varying positions of power and sensitivity. I believe you uncovered a document that mentioned only a few cryptic words: *Poulaine* and *Charles Audley* and *cryptographer*." At Phinney's nod, he continued. "This will provide an excellent example. A high-ranking French agent named Didier Poulaine came to England in `12 to kidnap our best cryptographer, Sir Charles Audley." He turned to the children. "Do you know what a cryptographer does?"

"A cryptographer deciphers codes," Elise said. "I know his name. Sir Charles is working on the Rosetta Stone."

"Yes, he is. He also creates codes for our armies. When we capture coded documents, he *breaks* the enemy code so we can read their communications. He is the best, and the French wanted to stop him. Poulaine captured him. He would have killed Audley, but one of our spies and a French double agent, a woman who is now married to Sir Charles, foiled him. Poulaine learned of Sir Charles' identity and location from Jacques Saultsein. Poulaine died before we could take him into custody, and we were frustrated by the knowledge that his information came from the very halls of our government. However, with the evidence we now have, we know who supplied that information to Saultsein and thus Poulaine, and we can prosecute those people as traitors."

"We have broken Saultsein's web. We can now track the various strands and eliminate any further leaks."

"Temporarily," Hargreaves hedged.

"Yes, temporarily," Sir Roger agreed, "for there are always more spiders to stamp out. Yet we can watch for the new spider and stop him before his web becomes large and tangled. Jacques Saultsein will have no successor to replace him."

"And Richard Malbury?" Phinney asked. "The son of a member of the House of Lords? What will become of him?"

"Unfortunately for him, the few documents we perused contain proofs of multiple actions that will lead to his conviction for treason against the Crown." He tucked the monocle into a little pocket of his grey brocaded waistcoat.

"And *Grandpére*?" Elise slid off the bench and crossed to her aunt, placing her little hand on Phinney's shoulder. "What of him? I don't want *Grandpére* to die."

The men didn't respond.

Phinney reached up to grasp Elise's hand. "The children have lost their parents, Sir Roger. Their home was burned. We've lived pillar to post for almost two years. Is there a way to avoid not only the death of their grandfather but also the destruction of their family name, which is the little remaining to them? I do not think *M'sieur* DeChambeaux knew of the murders of his son and daughter-in-law until it was a *fait accompli*."

"He would thereafter have feared for his own life," Mrs. Stowbridge added, "for that is the way Jack Salsby controlled people. *M'sieur* DeChambeaux would fear for his own life and the lives of any family remaining to him. The children's age would not have stopped Mr. Salsby. Mr. Montjoy can corroborate this."

"He offered that very comment, ma'am, to explain his own association with Saultsein."

"Then you understand how ruthless and cruel he is. Was."

"The prime minister must make the decision—," Sir Roger began only to have his colleague finish, "but we will argue in favor of *M'sieur* DeChambeaux's exile. For the sake of the children and the family name."

"Will this be acceptable?" Sir Roger looked at Phinney then the children. Vic nodded, too, even though he wasn't part of the family. "Now, we have only a little more to conclude. The nature of our business means that we will have no public ceremony."

"No medals!" Hank crossed his arms and pouted.

"We don't want any public acknowledgement," Elise said although her brother clearly disagreed.

"We prefer to live quietly," Mrs. Stowbridge affirmed.

"Indeed," Phinney added, "I would not want any of our names to be mentioned in public or in a sealed document or behind closed doors."

"You make it difficult for us to acknowledge your service."

"What did Constable Hoppock say?"

Hargreaves turned to Vic. "Why do you ask? What do you think he would say?"

"He *might* have said he was doing his duty as a constable, but I think he did it for Phinney. To keep her safe."

"That is indeed what he said."

Sir Roger fingered the gold chain of his monocle. "We can ensure the government provides you a quiet life, but you must accept a little recognition. Medals, certainly," he nodded at Hank who gave a whoop. The old man fought a smile. "A small ceremony with the Prime Minister at Buckingham Palace."

"The king and queen?" Elise breathed.

"Will the Prince Regent serve?"

"He will serve very well," her aunt said sternly.

"And a small monetary gift for you all, a token of the government's appreciation as well as a small compensation for what you had to endure. All of you," Hargreaves included with a nod to Mrs. Stowbridge and another to Orion and a third to Vic and Hank on the window bench.

"And Constable Hoppock?" Phinney asked.

"Certainly," Sir Roger said. His thumb pushed the gold chain into the pocket with the monocle. "Hargreaves, have you anything more?"

"No, sir. Mrs. Stowbridge, Miss Darracott, may I return in three days? We will set forward a good plan for your compensation."

"The children may wish to visit their grandfather."

"No," Elise said decidedly. "No, Phinney, I don't want him dead, but I also don't want to see him. He knew … ."

"Hank?"

"I'm with Elise."

"Very good," Hargreaves judged. "In three days then. Ladies, gentlemen," and they left, Orion opening the door then shutting it while everyone else managed only mute stares at each other.

"What do they mean, *compensation*?" Elise whispered.

"I don't care," Hank said. "I'm getting a medal."

"Money, I think," Phinney answered. "We might afford a roof over our heads."

"But you must stay with us," Mrs. Stowbridge protested.

"Or nearby," Elise said, "for we all have things to learn."

. ~ . ~ . ~ .

Phinney felt dazed by the rapid events of the past days.

Counting back, she scarcely believed that only two days ago she had walked to work in a vain hope to find evidence of murder. Then she met Conrad. She witnessed a murder. Someone tracked her through London's streets. Then came last night: her fight with Malbury, taken captive by Montjoy, and the moments of terror when Jack Salsby threatened the children. Then Conrad and Olivia and Orion arrived.

Unreal, parts of it. Other parts, terrifying.

The door burst open. "Phinney?"

She sprang from her chair. "Conrad!"

He rushed to her and swept her into his arms. She laughed with delight—dazed yet again but for a happier reason.

"I'm going to kiss you, Josephine Elizabeth Darracott."

"I'm waiting, Plow Boy."

The kiss was neither quick nor chaste and thoroughly delighted her.

After, she traced his lips with her fingertips. The strange stasis had lifted. Her old friends would be scandalized when she informed them—

after months of silence—that she had married the plowboy from Brize Norton.

"I have a new assignment. I informed the chief you would help me with it."

"You informed the chief? He didn't tell you?"

"He told me the assignment. I said you would help. It's about Jack Salsby's files."

"Didn't Chief Evans turn those over to Sir Roger Nazenby and his colleague—what was his name?"

"It's glad I am to hear the son of the Marquess of Grasmere made little impression upon you. They did receive some files, everything not dated this year. I showed them the cache Mrs. Stowbridge had taken the documents from. For a spymaster, Salsby kept neat records. Nazenby's men are searching the whole house. May even dismantle it. We have the recent files."

"What is the work I am to help you with? What do you think to find in the files?"

"Names. Locations. Likely in code. I know your worth, Phinney Darracott. You love a puzzle, and these files may give you some tricky ones. Once we pinpoint people, we'll arrest them and discover what information they have and how they got it. After we get settled, of course."

"Settled?"

"Married."

"Is this a proposal?"

"Well, I'd be on bended knee, but I'm liking you on my lap too much. But if you insist—."

She looped her arms around his neck. "Don't you dare. I like this, too. And I like the idea of working with you, the two of us."

The arm around her waist tightened. "That's right, the two of us working together. Only we won't start with two, will we? We'll be starting with five."

Phinney drew back then realized he counted the children. Their inclusion bloomed in her heart. "I can explain about Vic."

"Later. Right now, here's the important thing," and he gave her another kiss that curled her toes. "I've wanted to do that since I was fifteen," he confided. "Took a year to get my nerve up."

"At your fifteen, I would have been fourteen, and my father would have caned you."

"As long as he doesn't cane me out of heaven for daring to marry the vicar's daughter."

She pressed a quick kiss to his chin. "I may not need the bended knee, Conrad Hoppock, but I would like the words."

"After I kiss you again, Phinney Darracott."

Few words were spoken in the next quarter-hour.

. ~ . ~ . ~ .

Notes for Readers

Research for a historical novel is tricky. We writers want to increase the verisimilitude of our story, but we also want free rein to create that story. Real people may interact with our fictional inventions; fictional places may be woven into the patchwork of a real city. In *The Hazard for Spies*, curious readers will find actual places like Gentleman Jackson's alongside fictional places like Kirkgardie Street.

Government buildings in London have been located on Whitehall Street since the mid-1700s. The Home Office is tasked with the safety and protection of Britain, not only of the population but also the government's continuation. The spy-catching department run by Sir Roger Nazenby is my own invention as is Sir Roger himself, but such departments could be associated with the Home Office. Also my invention is the special Constabulary task force and Chief Constable Hector Evans who heads the force.

1814 is a year of hope for many in Europe. Not even the brilliant tactician that Napoleon was could survive his disastrous invasion of Russia. He surrendered to Coalition forces in March 1814, and in April he abdicated in favor of his son Napoleon II. Then he was banished to Elba in the Mediterranean Sea—only to escape a year later, March 1815. He reclaimed his title as emperor, raised a new army, and had 100 days of rule ... only to be defeated by the 7th Coalition, including the Duke of Wellington leading the British forces, at the battle of Waterloo on 18 June 1815. Thereafter, the British exiled him to the remote island of St. Helena in the south Atlantic, sufficiently far enough away that Europe felt safe. He died there, some say of stomach cancer and some say of arsenic poisoning, on 5 May 1821.

Napoleon's army located the Rosetta Stone—which is not originally a language-learning application. A French soldier "discovered" the carved stone in July 1799 while stationed in Egypt. I have often wondered if the stone were located originally near the great library of Alexandria which was burned by Julius Caesar in 48 BCE. It may have been moved to the lesser library of Serapeum, itself destroyed in 391 CE, and kept locally over the centuries until recognized as important by a French soldier with more than gold in his eyes. Although the French military tried to keep possession of the stone, the British took control of it at Alexandria in 1801. The Royal Navy transported it to London where it was placed on public display at the British Museum in 1802.

The Rosetta Stone is an ancient decree by the Egyptian pharaoh

Ptolemy V. The decree is written in three languages: ancient Greek, the Egyptian demotic, and Egyptian hieroglyphics. This stone decoded the mysterious hieroglyphics that had stumped scholars for centuries. I credit Sir Charles Audley with decoding part of the Rosetta Stone—that is purely my invention, for the purposes of the fifth **Hearts in Hazard** novel, *The Danger for Spies*. I enjoyed the characters of Eugenie DesChamps and Charles Audley so much that I wanted to mention them here in my farewell to the conflict of French spies.

Finally ~~ Mentioned numerous times in this story are press gangs in Liverpool and the murders at Parton March. Vic, Elise and Hank along with Phinney are introduced in *The Hazard of Secrets*, book 10 of the **Hearts in Hazard** series. In wrapping up this novel, popping out of my brain were snippets for another story with the children, much older, using the life and death skills that they chose at the end of this book. It could happen—but other characters are clamoring more loudly for their stories to be told. Vic, Elise, and Hank with his knife skills must wait.

Thank You!

Thank you for reading *The Hazard for Spies*. We're approaching the end of the Hearts in Hazard series. Dreaming up the series in 2013, I never expected to fall in love with every one of the twelve books. I'm experiencing a strange sadness :: "Don't go yet," the series calls.

The last projected book of Hearts in Hazard, book 12, is *The Hazard of Hearts*, my reproduction of the vintage gothic ~ *Two wives haunt the castle. Will she be the third to die?*

For any questions, comments, and speculations, please contact winkbooks@aol.com. You can find my books on my Amazon author page or my website ~~ www.writersinkbooks.com

To receive monthly information about all of my books, please join my monthly newsletter list. Contact me at winkbooks@aol.com and receive a free peek at the book I am currently writing. I won't pester you with affiliate links or pass your email to any other person or institution. Promise.

Indie writers thrive on reviews. With *any* book that you enjoy, please share with other readers looking for escape from the stresses of life.

Dream it. Believe it. Do it.
~~ *M.A. Lee*

Hearts in Hazard by M.A. Lee

Mysteries with a dash of romance, set during the Regency Era of England

1 ~ *A Game of Secrets* ~ Smugglers, secrets and spies: Kate tries to hide in plain sight; Tony tries to catch a spy. First they fall in love, then they fall into trouble with smugglers. Will they survive?

2 ~ *A Game of Spies* ~ Salons and soirées, flirtation and dancing, gambling and spies: Josette and Giles fall in love over a deck of cards—and try not to die.

Spymaster Giles Hargreaves was introduced in *A Game of Secrets*.

3 ~ *A Game of Hearts* ~ **Two couples** :: One titled widow, one wealthy businessman: two hearts shadowed by their past. One bright young flirt, one hard-edged young man: two hearts crossed by circumstance. Mix in a courtesan and two rakes, all out for mischief, and murder bloody and foul.

4 ~ *The Danger of Secrets* ~ Deep in the wintry countryside, a house warmed by relatives and friends: secrets of family, secrets of hearts, secrets of blood and pain. Match a daughter to an unknown father; match a spinster to an earl; match a serial killer to his next victim.

Gordon Musgrove was introduced in *A Game of Spies*.

5 ~ *The Danger for Spies* ~ Impossibilities? Rakes don't lose their hearts. Spies don't give up the game. No one hides in plain sight. Codes are unbreakable. A man can't hold onto revenge for years and years. Impossibilities are designed to be shattered.

Toby Kennitt was introduced in *A Game of Spies*.

6 ~ *The Danger to Hearts* ~ A country manor in early Spring: older woman and younger man. Horses, cats, needlework, roses and afternoon teas ~ What could possibly go wrong in an idyll? Trouble in the past, trouble now, and murder.

The character Jess Carter was introduced in *A Game of Secrets*.

7 ~ *The Key to Secrets* ~ Debutantes should snare fiancés, not murder them. Constable Hector Evans must solve three murders. Is his former love guilty, of is she a convenient scapegoat?

Constable Hector Evans was introduced in *The Danger to Hearts*.

8 ~ *The Key for Spies* ~ Spies and traitors. Lies and treachery. Unexpected love where bullets fly. One traitor destroys loyalty. What will two traitors destroy?

9 ~ *The Key for Hearts* ~ A convenient marriage inconveniently causes murder.

10 ~ *The Hazard of Secrets*. Two hearts with dangerous pasts—Can they keep their secrets, or will murder force them to reveal all?

Constable Hector Evans, elevated to chief constable, has a cameo appearance.

11 ~ *The Hazard for Spies* ~ Disguised to spy. Will murder destroy their chance for love?

Chief Constable Hector Evans has a cameo appearance.

12 ~ *The Hazard for Hearts* ~ Two wives haunt the castle. Will she be the third to die?

M.A. Lee also writes the **Into Death** Series, set after World War

I

Digging into Death ~ A governess seeking refuge, a handsome young man, an archaeological dig: romance is inevitable; murder is not. Suspicions escalate, artifacts are stolen, and then a second murder. Has the love of her life beguiled her straight into death? Available in paperback and e-book

Christmas with Death ~ Christmas is for miracles, merriment, and murder. Set in 1919 at an English country manor for a party throughout Christmastide. Available in paperback and e-book.

Portrait with Death, publishing soon ~ the conclusion of the Isabella Newcombe series

Nonfiction by M.A. Lee

Think like a Pro Writer series

1 ~ Think like a Pro: New Advent for Writers ~ Seven lessons to guide your growth from newbie writer to "thinking like a pro writer". Now available in paperback and e-book.

2 ~ Think / Pro: A Planner for Writers ~ An undated planner with daily word counts, progress meters, project planning, and goals analysis. Paperback only. How else will you record your goals and progress?

3 ~ Old Geeky Greeks: Write Stories with Ancient Techniques ~ Storytelling has its roots in the strong foundations of classical antiquity. Avoid the re-packaged "exclusive insights" and "wham-pow webinars" and return to the source, organized as a seminar in book form.

4 ~ Discovering Your Novel ~ a 52-week course for new writers, offering guidance from original idea to publication and marketing.

5 ~ Discovering Characters ~ Delving deeply into your primary characters entails more than just templates and character interviews. You also need to know your secondary characters. Focus on more than appearance, more than intellect, and explore your characters hearts and souls. Discover them!

6 ~ Discovering Your Plot ~ What writers need and want for plot structures and genre expectations. Control pacing, tension, and suspense with a stronger comprehension of the major sections of a novel.

7 ~ Discovering your Author Brand ~ The greatest secret to catch the attention of fly-by readers? Branding. Writers need to brand their books, their series, and themselves as the author. Packed with examples and explanations from past successful marketing efforts.

8 ~ Discovering Sentence Craft ~ Zeug-what? Chiasmus? Auxesis? Are those spelled correctly? Well, yes. These are literary devices used for centuries by the best writers to make their works memorable. Writers are artists, seeking ideas from the creative muse. We're also crafters, looking for the best ways to present those creative ideas. DiscS~Craft presents techniques for using figurative & interpretive concepts as well as the structures of inversions, repetitions, oppositions, and sequencings.

Just Start Writing :: Inspiration 4 Writers, book 1 ~Writing can be a dizzy whirl of a carousel, all colors and mirrors with unicorns and griffins and dragons to ride. How do you get your ticket, climb on the carousel, and join the writing ride? If you want to pursue your writing dream, Just Start Writing will help you start.

2 * 0 * 4 Lifestyle series

2 * 0 * 4 Lifestyle: A Planner for Living ~ Intermittent fasting. Bible Journaling. Keto Diet. 7-Minute Workout. Five minutes with God. If the newest fads to follow are leaving you cold and edgy, time to re-think your daily plan. Return to Luke 10:27 to involve the whole self—heart, soul, mind & body. 2 * 0 * 4 offers an undated planner to help you muse and move, feast and fast, and live and love. Paperback only. How else will you write in it? Available in the Meadow and the Mountain River editions.

Pen Names of M.A. Lee

Remi Black ~ Fae Mark'd

The Fae Mark'd Wizard
Weave a Wizardry Web
Dream a Deadly Dream
Sing a Graveyard Song
Kindle a Fae's Wrath (coming soon)
Quench a Dragon's Fire (in the sketching stage)
Dance to Bone-Edged Music (in the sketching stage)

Fae Mark'd World
To Wield the Wind :: Spells of Air 1
To Charm the Air: Spells of Air 2 (coming soon)
To Curse the Wyre: Spells of Air 3 (sketching stage)

Edie Roones ~ Seasons in Sansward

Summer Sieges
Autumn Spells
Winter Sorcery
Spring Magicks (in the sketching stage)

All Writers Ink Books are available at Amazon and other online distributors.

For comments, questions, and speculations, contact
winkbooks@aol.com.
Use the subject line to direct your email to a specific book or series.

Thank you!

www.ingramcontent.com/pod-product-compliance
Lightning Source LLC
Chambersburg PA
CBHW020648180626
46816CB00003B/1185